HOUSE OF STORMS
AND SECRETS

HR MOORE

Titles by HR Moore:

The Relic Trilogy:
Queen of Empire
Temple of Sand
Court of Crystal

In the Gleaming Light

The Ancient Souls Series:
Nation of the Sun
Nation of the Sword
Nation of the Stars

Shadow and Ash Duology:
Kingdoms of Shadow and Ash
Dragons of Asred (coming early 2023)

Shadow and Ash stories:
The Water Rider and the High Born Fae
House of Storms and Secrets

http://www.hrmoore.com

Part One

Chapter One

STORM HURRIED ALONG THE castle's wide corridor. Her chores—always a terrifying list—had doubled since the arrival of the fallen angels. She had scant time to clean the kitchen before Cook returned from her break, not that Storm ever got a break, this just one of the many injustices in her life.

Moaning permeated Storm's whirling thoughts, and her feet froze in place. Her eyes sought the source, scanning the alcoves, along with the shadows cast by the tall, carved columns. Her insides plummeted when she found the Queen of the Western Kingdom of Fairy Land partially hidden in an alcove, a man lavishing attention on her half-visible breasts.

Fuck. Storm had to get out of here before …

Queen Rosalind opened her eyes, which were misty, at least until she realized she had an audience. Then rage burned the haze away.

Fuck. Fuck. Fuck.

The Queen pulled the man off her. He began to protest, but then he saw Storm, spluttered some unintelligible words, and scurried off along the corridor. Storm wasn't really sure who he was; one of the Queen's many attractive male advisors, perhaps.

'You dare spy on your Queen?' said Rosalind, her tone low and menacing. Pink stained her cheeks, and Storm wondered at that. Surely she wasn't embarrassed? The whole castle knew of her frequent sexual exploits.

'Of course not,' Storm replied, her tone, as always, too sharp for her station. 'Your Majesty,' she added, with a bow of her head, 'I …'

'Get out of my way.'

Storm pressed herself against the stone wall and bowed her head low. 'I'm sorry, Your Majesty,' she murmured, as Rosalind swept past with a swish of fine fabric.

The Queen marched away, her heels clicking against the stone, and Storm rolled her eyes. *You're welcome.*

Storm watched until the Queen's tall, stick-like form had clicked to the far end of the lengthy stone corridor, past countless portraits of long-forgotten royals and empty suits of armor. Only when the ornate double doors of the Queen's bedchamber had closed behind her did Storm dare to make a sound. She wasn't scared of the dreadful woman, but it was a fool's game to court punishment.

She headed for a thick tapestry that depicted a particularly gruesome hunting scene and thrust it aside to reveal a set of steep, dark stairs. The Queen kept any hint of the castle's unsightly underbelly firmly hidden. She didn't like to be reminded of her dependence on others to keep her in perfectly pressed silk pajamas and shimmering diamonds.

Storm fumed as she stomped down the steps, cheering herself by considering the virtues of various methods of regicide. Perhaps a drop or two of poison—the Queen's preferred method of dispatching others—wouldn't that be ironic …

Storm chuckled as she reached the bottom, so preoccupied she almost ran headlong into a pair of jet-black wings.

She came to an abrupt halt, and her mind went blank. 'Gabriel,' she whispered, the breath whooshing from her lungs.

He whirled to face her, and she met his gaze, his features dark and devastatingly handsome. Her mouth went dry as they took each other in. 'I ...'

'Storm,' he said, with a curt incline of his head, his voice a sensual purr that sent a shiver down her spine. And then he was gone, with only the barest whisper of his outermost wing feather across the back of her hand.

'Storm?' said Hunter, rushing to her side. He was big and burly, used to carrying deer carcasses through the woods. That meant there wasn't much she could do to protest as he pulled her short, curvy frame into the enormous kitchen, snatched up an apple, and made her take a bite. 'Are you okay?'

She wasn't sure what she was. This whole damnable situation was fraying her edges. 'I'm fine,' she said, shooing him away and taking a seat at the scarred wooden table. It was littered with sage and rosemary, apples and garlic peelings. A divine smell emanated from the oven, but the cook made a point of leaving every last bit of mess for Storm.

'I'll make tea,' said Hunter, plucking a handful of mint leaves through the open window. But he didn't turn back.

'Hunter?' said Storm, noting the rigid set of his shoulders.

'By *The Powers*,' he said, his eyes fixed on something outside.

Storm jumped up. 'What is it?'

'Shush,' he whispered. 'He's doing it *again*.'

'What …? Oh …' Gabriel—the leader of the fallen angel menace—was smuggling another of his angels out of the dungeons. So that's what he was doing here …

Gabriel had forged a fragile bond with the Queen, mostly based on him fucking her, as far as anyone could tell, but the Queen was fond of exerting her authority whenever she got the chance. This mostly comprised of her locking up Gabriel's deputies, but Gabriel, seemingly unconcerned about the consequences, always freed them at his earliest convenience and told the Queen they'd escaped.

'He can't get away with this,' said Hunter, bringing his closed fist down on the windowsill. The gesture was furious yet controlled, Hunter careful not to draw Gabriel's attention. 'The Queen might be a spiteful old ball of wretchedness, but the fallen angel scum are spitting in her face … in *our* faces!'

Storm tore her eyes from Gabriel and met Hunter's livid gaze. 'Yes,' she said with a shrug, because what else was there to say?

'You have to tell the Queen. You're the only one who can.'

Storm's mouth dropped open. 'You do remember she treats me like I'm muck on the bottom of her most favorite shoes?'

'She can't make your life worse than it already is, and you're the only one she can't get rid of. Your father …' Hunter stopped abruptly, not wanting to veer into painful territory, but he raised his eyebrows, daring her to argue. Of course, he was right.

Storm was the daughter of the Queen's former lover, and the Queen had promised him—on his death bed—that she would look after his only child. His death had sealed the vow, and no matter how many times the Queen had tried to break it, the magic held firm.

Hunter narrowed his gaze. 'Unless you're too chicken …'

Storm scowled at him. 'How old are you?'

'Or maybe you have a soft spot for the angels and their big, muscular chests.'

'You've noticed,' said Storm. 'I thought you would have.'

Hunter made a hissing noise like an angry cat, and Storm made a face. 'I should run away,' she said, casting her eyes at the now empty vista through the window. 'Anything would be better than this hellhole.'

Hunter's features turned skeptical. 'But where would you go?'

Storm rolled her eyes. Another world. That's where she would go. Far, far away.

Hunter shoved her short frame towards the door. 'Off you go. You need to get to her before Gabriel works her into a muscle-induced trance.'

The image made Storm want to vomit. Big, beautiful Gabriel laying so much as a finger on Rosalind … well, she didn't want to think about it.

* * *

The Powers That Be hated her. That was the only conclusion Storm could come to as she slipped into the Queen's bedchamber, through white doors covered in gilt swirls. She scanned her eyes across the opulent room decorated in purple and gold, with crushed velvet drapes and cushions, a bed raised on a circular platform, and an enormous mirror off to one side.

Storm had knocked, but there had been no answer, so she'd entered as quietly as she could, her footsteps muffled by her soft leather shoes.

Storm's mouth fell open at the scene she found: Gabriel's dark, shirtless form prowling towards the Queen, whose eyes were glued to the angel. Storm's feet rooted to the spot. She knew she should make her presence known, or retreat, but ... could this really be happening twice in one day?

'Another one escaped,' said Gabriel. He stopped in front of the Queen, who sat on a throne-like chair near a floor-to-ceiling window.

'How annoying,' Rosalind breathed. She leaned forward and ran a hand down his rippling chest. He bent and kissed her neck, and the Queen shivered. Gabriel chuckled, then bit her, his wings unfurling, spanning half the width of the room with their huge length.

The Queen gasped, sinking her hands into his dark locks, and a choked sound escaped Storm's lips. She clamped her hands over her mouth as she realized what she'd done. She should flee, but it was fascinating, in the way of a horror story.

Gabriel reluctantly released the Queen, watching Storm with a blank expression, his wings pulsing minutely behind him.

'Yes?' said the Queen, as though Storm was a cockroach she wanted to step on.

'My Queen,' said Storm. She sent another glace in Gabriel's direction, wishing she could disappear into the door frame.

The Queen's hard eyes bored into her. 'Get on with it.'

'Ah ... um ... there's been another ... incident ... with the fallen,' said Storm. Her eyes flicked once again to Gabriel.

'Another one escaped,' the Queen snapped. 'Gabriel informed me.'

'He let it go,' said Storm, quickly, before the Queen could dismiss her.

The Queen raised an eyebrow, then swung her head to Gabriel. 'Did he?' she said slowly. She rolled the words around her mouth as though delighted.

The corners of Gabriel's lips twitched upward, creating the beginnings of a smirk. 'I would never do that, Your Majesty,' he said with a half bow.

'As I thought,' said the Queen. 'You dare slander my beloved concubine?'

'Your Majesty,' Storm spluttered, 'I …' *Concubine?*

'Leave,' said the Queen, then she yanked Gabriel back into her arms.

'How'd it go?' asked Hunter, as Storm appeared at the bottom of the servants' stairs once more.

So many emotions screwed tight in her chest: loathing, revulsion, disappointment. It made her queasy. 'As well as you'd expect,' she said, then pulled Hunter towards the exit. He tried to ask more, but she ignored his questions, her mind replaying the images of Gabriel kissing and *biting* the Queen over and over. Her guts roiled.

Storm had a million tasks to complete, for everyone from the cook to the gardener to the blacksmith, but something inside her had snapped. Seeing them in the flesh was so much worse than anything she'd imagined. How could Gabriel do it?

They passed under a stone arch and out into the castle's kitchen garden. The smells of sage and lemon balm wafted around them, but the carefully curated beauty was no match for Storm's wild, dark thoughts.

They headed deep into the woods, pushing aside brambles and nettles, and stepping over decaying tree trunks covered with moss. The sound of birdsong increased as they walked, for even the birds disliked the angels; they'd been avoiding the castle since the fallen had arrived. Which was when, exactly? Storm couldn't even pinpoint how long they'd been here, but it seemed like an eternity.

Storm's shoulders finally fell as they crossed the boundary, leaving the Queen's land and heading deeper into the Enchanted Forest. It should have been oppressive, heading into the gloom, but to Storm it was liberating, for the castle and its grounds—everything the Queen owned—was a gilded prison.

'It's like she doesn't care,' said Storm eventually, slowing her pace to a trudge.

Hunter let out a long breath, seeming relieved the silence was over. 'At least you tried.'

'I just wish I knew why they were here. What they want … what the Queen wants.'

'She wants adoration,' said Hunter, 'and Gabriel provides that in spades.'

'Gabriel,' said Storm, through gritted teeth. 'Her *concubine*. He's surely plotting her downfall.'

'If he is, the Queen will know.'

Storm laughed at the sincerity in his tone. 'Your faithful adoration is a little strange, considering you supposedly hate her.'

'She's a sad, lonely old witch,' said Hunter, giving Storm a playful shove, 'but she's a canny, sad, lonely old witch; I give credit where it's due.'

'There's nothing sad or lonely about her,' said Storm. She shoved him back, and the darkness receded a little.

Hunter stumbled into a dwarf tree, one of seven set out in a circle around a clearing, and its lowest branch swayed wildly.

'Careful,' she said, 'or the dwarf magic will get you.'

Hunter chuckled. 'You do love a fiction ... these trees are as friendly as friendly can be.'

Hunter dropped down to sit under the biggest of the seven trees. They were a dwarf variety, but had grown so tall, the tips reached towards the clouds. No one knew why. Magic, presumably.

Hunter patted the grass beside him. She sat, leaning her head against him, and he hooked an arm around her. 'I'm not sure I can go back, Hunter,' she said after a long pause.

He stiffened. 'Where would you go?'

'Somewhere I'm not a slave.'

'You're not a slave here.'

Storm met his gaze, her forehead furrowed.

'Okay, maybe you lack some conventional freedoms, but ...'

'But what? I should accept my position and be grateful for the scraps the Queen throws me?'

'No, that's not ...'

'Then what?' she asked, putting space between them.

'Well ... isn't there something simple about your life? Something steady?'

Storm scowled. 'Before the Queen came along, I ...' She screwed up her face, trying to remember her life before. 'My father ... he ...'

'He was a good man, by all accounts,' said Hunter, in an obvious bid to take the wind from her sails.

'I don't want to talk about it,' said Storm, 'but I know there's more out there for me, if only I'm brave enough to find it.'

Storm looked away, and silence descended again.

'Hey, I'm sorry,' said Hunter. He reached for her and pulled her back to his side.

Storm rolled her eyes and rested her head against him. She could never stay mad at Hunter for long, for he was all she had in this world, and he meant well.

'Of course you deserve more,' he said. 'Maybe I'm being selfish, but I don't want to lose you.'

'I don't want to lose you either,' said Storm, inhaling his familiar woodsy scent. A blue tit pecked around the base of the tree. It was surprisingly brave, passing so close she could reach out and touch it.

'Oh, to be a bird,' said Storm.

'Or not,' said Hunter, his head turned up to the sky.

Storm followed his gaze to where a hawk circled overhead. 'A metaphor for my life,' said Storm.

She tracked the songbird as it explored the base of the tree, willing the hawk to fly away. The hawk remained, but the tit disappeared before her eyes. She sat bolt upright, casting her eyes around. 'Did you see that?'

'What?' said Hunter, an edge of unease in his tone.

'The blue tit. It's … gone!'

Hunter scoffed as he turned to get a better look, his face saying he was certain the bird would be there. But it wasn't. He put his hand into the roots, pressing down as though to stand, but with no warning, the soil gave way, and they fell backwards, down down down, into the ground.

Chapter Two

STORM LANDED WITH A thud, and the air flew from her lungs. She gasped and wheezed, trying to catch a breath, everything about her surroundings disorientating.

Only a few chinks of light made it through the mass of brown roots above, and packed earth rested beneath her fingers. They seemed to have fallen into an underground burrow of sorts, although the roots were a long way above … she didn't dare to think what animal would make a burrow such as this …

Storm turned her head, and could see Hunter's outline nearby. He seemed to be in a similar state, breathing hard. That was good; he was alive at least.

And then a dim, yellowish light illuminated the space. A light seeming to come from a stone held in the hands of … what in the Seven Hells?

A short, squat man hovered over Hunter, nudging him with his boot.

'Leave him alone,' said Storm, trying and failing to get up.

'Now, now,' said a short, squat woman. She'd appeared next to Storm out of nowhere. 'No need for any of that. We're all friends here.'

'Then why are we winded and on the floor?' said Storm.

'Easiest way to get you down here,' said the woman.

'We're rusty, see,' said the man. 'Haven't had much practice these past few years.'

'These past few hundred years,' corrected the woman. 'I'm Gamble, and this is Luck. Pleased to make your acquaintance.'

'Likewise,' Hunter wheezed, ever well-mannered, although his voice sounded unsure.

Gamble and Luck helped them to their feet. The woman had a kindly face with sharp, shrewd eyes. Her brown hair—tied back in a bun—was almost half grey, her mud-colored dress sensible and worn, her belly round. The man's face was anything but kind, although Storm sensed he was more bark than bite.

'Come along,' said Gamble. 'Can't stand gaping.' She ushered them through a hole in the mess of tree roots, into a dark, dank, earthen corridor.

'Where are we going?' asked Storm.

'You'll see,' said Gamble, pulling out a second glow stone to light their way.

'Patience,' said Luck.

'Why not just tell us?' said Storm.

'Reveal yer secrets, an' you lose yer mystique,' said Luck, with a wink.

'How'd giving up yer secrets work for *you*?' asked Gamble, with a meaningful eyebrow raise.

Storm sighed. It hadn't worked out well for her at all … had resulted in the loss of all she held dear, in fact.

'She ain't given up *all* her secrets though, has she?' Luck said with a chuckle.

'What do you mean?' asked Hunter. He threw a curious look in Storm's direction.

Gamble and Luck laughed.

'He's an 'andsome one, I'll give you that,' said Gamble, nudging Storm.

'And she ain't too shoddy-looking neither,' said Luck, wiggling his eyebrows at Hunter.

'Where are we?' said Storm, in a desperate bid to divert the pesky creatures. Why did people always feel the need to speculate about her relationship with Hunter?

Gamble and Luck shared another amused look, then Luck said, 'You'll see, Yer Majesty.'

Storm laughed nervously as they emerged into a room of sorts, sunlight poking through the sparse roots above. 'You're the first person to call me that in … well … in a long time.' The Queen had stamped out the use of Storm's title almost immediately after her father— the King of the South West of Fairy Land—had died.

Storm tried to bring back the details, but it was difficult. Almost all her memories had become muddled since the angels had arrived … or maybe even before. She could barely remember the King's face, let alone exactly how the Queen had wrestled away all that should have belonged to Storm. All she could really recall was that the Queen had tricked her into handing over the keys to her kingdom, and Storm had regretted it every day since.

'Well, it's true though, ain't it?' said Gamble, defensively.

'I'm not sure any longer,' said Storm. 'The Queen and the angels …'

'Parasites,' said Gamble. 'Come down here, steal houses and food, cut down …'

'STOP!' shouted Luck. Everyone froze. 'Don't touch that.'

Hunter had roamed to the far corner of the space, his hand hovering above a small, mostly hidden well with roots growing all around.

'Why?' said Hunter, stepping back.

'Poison,' spat Gamble.

No one moved for a few beats, and then Gamble snapped to action as though nothing had happened. 'This way,' she said. She ushered them down another dark tunnel, brooking no argument.

They walked in silence, the ground increasingly uneven, the air thick with tension, until eventually the tunnel widened and lightened, the end in sight.

'Wow,' said Hunter, as they caught their first glimpse of what lay beyond. 'This is …'

'… unexpected,' Storm finished. They stepped out of the tunnel, and the opening disappeared under a blanket of vegetation behind them. 'What the …'

A fairy wearing a pouffy pink dress flew past. 'Hi Gamble, Luck,' said the fairy. 'Can't stop. Freaking godchildren. You know how it is. And I need to make it back in time for godmother commissioning!' Her words trailed behind her, fast and high-pitched, and then she was gone.

Godmother commissioning?

'Welcome to Via d'Magical,' said Gamble. 'The very heart of the Enchanted Forest.'

'Not usually so crowded,' said Luck. 'New crop of godmothers leaving school today.'

'Being assigned their first godchildren,' said Gamble, rubbing her hands together in glee.

'Can't wait to see who Phinella gets,' said Luck, raising his eyebrows.

'Youngest godmother ever,' explained Gamble.

'Top of the class.'

'Something of a celebrity.'

'Not to mention, easy on the eye,' added Luck. Gamble shoved him hard, and he scowled.

Storm and Hunter stared open-mouthed at the bustling underground street. The air was abuzz with pixies, fairies, snapdragons, and sprites, while witches, hobgoblins, dryads, and nymphs packed the cobbles.

A tavern with swing doors dominated the corner of the street, griffins, unicorns, and a large, scary-looking cat with three tails drinking from water troughs outside. And at the far end, past an intriguing array of shops, stood an impressive marble building with wide steps, ornate columns, and a tall fountain outside.

'By *The Powers* …' said Storm. 'What is this place?'

'Via d'Magical,' Luck slowly repeated, as though she were stupid.

'Where magical folk come for gossip and supplies,' said Gamble. She gave Luck a warning look.

'Why have you brought us here?' said Hunter, narrowly avoiding the hindquarters of a centaur.

'Patience, young'en,' said Luck, then he strode off up the street.

Gabriel stalked up and down the line of angels, flexing his wings menacingly behind him. 'Well?' he snapped. He couldn't wait to leave this hellhole, and wasn't above taking out his frustration on those he'd brought with him.

'We're approaching the border,' said a scrawny-looking angel. Gabriel couldn't recall his name.

'And?'

'Nothing,' said a short angel with ginger wings.

'Nothing,' Gabriel repeated, somehow resisting the temptation to punch a tree. Gods spare him. He'd lived a long and arduous life, but this … *test* might finally see to his demise.

'And we're approaching the border,' the scrawny angel repeated. He looked at the tree line off to their right.

'If we don't get permission to dig further, we'll soon have to stop,' said the ginger.

'You saw what happened to Henri when he tried to go over,' said scrawny.

Gabriel suppressed the almost overwhelming urge to rip out both of their jugulars. 'You may leave,' he said, dismissing the line of angels with a flick of his hand.

Only Michael remained; the only one he could trust. Silence settled for a beat as Michael leaned his tall, lithe form back against a great oak tree, his black wings folded behind him. 'Is she responding?' he said, watching Gabriel carefully.

Gabriel shook his head.

'What about the poisoned apple for Rosalind?'

Gabriel shook his head again. 'I have a plan, although …' he trailed off. 'I don't know if it will work.'

Michael huffed out a breath and crossed his arms, then addressed the true cause of Gabriel's bad mood. 'She can't hold out much longer. It's been *months*.'

'You know what she's like. She'd hold out for eternity if it meant punishing me.' And if there was one thing Gabriel had learned during his time here, it was that the people of this world would fuck with his plans, no matter how carefully laid. How he longed to leave.

'You'll update Isaiah on our progress?' asked Michael.

Gabriel nodded. 'I will go to the House of Portals now.'

Storm gaped as they walked up Via d'Magical, the sights both wonderful and absurd. Fruits and vegetables floated in the windows of greengrocers, chocolatiers displayed impossibly intricate constructions of windmills and fairy wings, and the apothecary was full to bursting with oddly shaped glass bottles, and crystal formations in perfect spheres.

A hand grabbed the back of Storm's threadbare dress and tugged. She barely had time to make sense of it before her back landed against something hard, a hand coming to rest over her mouth.

Storm scowled at Gamble, trying to wrench free of the woman's iron grasp. 'What the ...'

'Shush,' Gamble hissed.

Storm followed Gamble's gaze out of the shadowy alleyway and across the street to where Queen Rosalind descended the grand marble steps.

'What is that place?' Storm whispered.

'Home of *The Powers That Be*,' said Luck. He raised an eyebrow, as though surprised she didn't know.

'What's the Queen doing there?' said Storm.

'Was going ter ask you the same question,' said Luck, his mistrustful eyes boring into hers.

Storm scowled. 'How would I know?'

'She doesn't tell Storm anything,' said Hunter. 'Treats her like a servant.'

'Hmmm,' said Luck, apparently unconvinced.

'Come on,' said Gamble, pulling them deeper into the alley. 'We're late.'

The dwarves led Hunter and Storm away from the main shopping street, through a series of increasingly seedy side streets. Storm tried to make sense of the day's surprising happenings, from her encounter with Gabriel, to being abducted by dwarves, to the Queen's visit to *The Powers*. Was the Queen still searching for a way to get rid of Storm? Was that why she was here?

They reached a dreary grey door in a ramshackle building that, like the whole area, had seen better days. Gamble rapped three times in quick succession, paused, then did four more, causing flecks of white paint to rain down from the doorjamb.

A judder of bolts sliding free vibrated through the door, then it swung inward, and the dwarves hurried them inside.

'About bloody time,' said a young female dwarf with blond hair and pale green eyes. She led them into a dingy, windowless room with a handful of upturned crates scattered around a makeshift table.

The building had an industrial feel, and Storm wondered about its purpose. Warehouse? Factory? Drugs den?

'Sit,' said the blond-haired dwarf. Storm wasn't sure if it was an invitation or an order, but she complied anyway.

'Sorry, Genelle, got caught up,' said Gamble.

Silence settled, and Storm leaned forward on her crate. She almost put her elbows on the table, but it was grimy, only the Gods knew what staining its surface, so she diverted them to her knees instead. 'What are we doing here?' she asked, looking to Genelle, who was apparently in charge.

'The Queen's working with the fallen angels,' said Genelle.

'No, really?' said Storm, her tone dripping with sarcasm.

'And we would like you to help us banish the angels from Fairy Land.'

Storm laughed, then threw a disbelieving look at Hunter.

'I told you,' said Hunter, 'the Queen hates Storm. Sorry …' he added, with an apologetic shrug in her direction.

'He's not lying,' said Storm. 'The Queen has tried to kill me many times. The only thing stopping her is the magical vow she made to my father before he died.'

'None of that means you can't help,' said Luck, testily. ''Less you're happy with angels digging up the Dark Forest, that is?'

'What?' said Hunter. 'They're doing what?'

'They've blown a whole section to smithereens,' said Genelle, 'and are digging too.'

'Looking for something,' said Gamble. 'Causing death and destruction. Creatures fleeing for their lives.'

'What are they looking for?' said Storm, her heart hammering in her chest. She was dying to know the angels' true purpose, and the Dark Forest sat at the very center of their world, sustained by ancient magic. Anything that threatened its health would ripple out and impact them all.

'Need you ter help us find out,' said Luck.

Storm's insides fell with disappointment. 'How are we supposed to do that?'

Genelle's features screwed into a look of abject disbelief. 'Are you kidding me? You live under the same roof as the Queen. The angels are there half the time … especially their leader. Open your eyes and ears and snoop around. Ask questions. Use your freaking minds and think of a way.'

'We need to know what the angels are looking for,' said Gamble, more kindly, 'an' what the Queen is getting out of it. Why's she working with them.'

'An' why did she visit *The Powers* just now?' added Luck, distrust still alight in his eyes.

'Something fishy going on with them for sure,' said Genelle.

Storm suppressed the urge to throw something. There was no way she could find out anything of use. The Queen would have Storm locked up if she caught her snooping. Or flayed. Or both. And the angels … they barely spoke to anyone. Spending time alone with them was virtually impossible. She should know; she tried regularly enough.

'Well?' said Genelle. 'Will you help us?'

Storm met Hunter's gaze. He shrugged. 'If they're truly cutting down parts of the forest, I'm in,' he said. 'That's my home and my hunting ground. It's always been in balance, but if those bastards are destroying it …' He balled his hands into fists. 'I'm in.'

Storm took a deep breath. She would probably regret this, but she nodded anyway, because, what else could she do? Return to her prison and live out the rest of her days beholden to the Queen? 'Okay.'

'Good,' said Genelle. 'We can talk tactics later, after the godmothers' commissioning ceremony. Something strange is going on with The King of Southern Fairy Land, or so the grapevine whispers.'

'Ooh, imagine if Phinella's assigned to Prince Florian,' said Luck. He leaned forward in his seat at the titillating notion. 'Would be *sensational*.'

'Why?' said Genelle.

'Oh, come on,' said Gamble, 'the columnists would have a field day. The dashing Prince of the Southern Lands paired with a young, beautiful godmother? They'd be a powerhouse. Celebrity …'

Genelle scowled as she cut Gamble off. 'Yes, well, I couldn't care less how they would look on the front pages of the tabloids. Could they help defeat the angels? That's all I care about. And it's all *you* should care about too.'

Chapter Three

GODMOTHERS AND THEIR GODCHILDREN *may not engage in romantic relationships of any kind.* The words played over and over in Gabriel's mind as he watched the happy scene unfolding before him. It was gold; Prince Florian's face buried in the bare cleavage of his newly appointed godmother, Phinella. How long had they been screwing? They certainly looked comfortable in the intimate embrace …

She'd become his godmother only yesterday, to much ooh-ing and ah-ing, their pairing all any news outlets could talk about. *Didn't they look wonderful together? Wasn't this a pairing of legend? Surely The Powers had foretold one of the most auspicious matches of all time.* No one would dare suggest they'd make a good romantic couple, for that was forbidden, but if evidence of such a scandal should get into the hands of the press? Well …

Gabriel suppressed the urge to laugh. Instead, he used the strange contraption in his hand to capture the moment. A blinding light flashed across the room, and the couple sprang apart.

'This is so much better than anticipated,' Gabriel said slowly. He'd hoped for something incriminating, but this …

Florian reached for his sword while Phinella rushed to cover herself, but the fight left their eyes when they saw what Gabriel held in his hand. Phinella sank back onto the bed.

'I'm glad you understand the gravity of your situation,' said Gabriel. He stepped into the room, taking in every detail of the opulent splendor, everything spick and span and gleaming. 'Luckily for you, I'm a reasonable man, and I'm confident we can come to an arrangement.'

'What do you want?' said Florian, his teeth clenched.

He was pluckier than Gabriel had expected, which made Gabriel feel almost bad for him … almost. 'In exchange for destroying this picture, and keeping the secret of your affair …'

'It's hardly an affair,' Florian retorted.

Gabriel tilted his head. Plucky, and easily provoked. 'Regardless,' he said, 'all I require in return is the procurement of one small and highly prized magical object.' He looked at them expectantly.

'Unbelievable,' said Phinella. She had a kind of magnetic glamour about her, and Gabriel couldn't blame Florian for his tryst. 'You want a poisoned apple, don't you? Rosalind's been after one for years.'

Gabriel inclined his head. 'I see why you were top of your year. If you ever want a proper job …'

'We can't get you an apple,' said Phinella, with a shake of her head. 'It's not possible.'

'Liar,' said Gabriel.

'I'm not …'

Gabriel held up a hand, and Phinella fell silent.

'I know there's a way; my informants have it on good authority.' The words were almost true. 'So if I were you, I'd get to work. I expect a progress report by midnight in three days, or this picture will find its way to the press.' He held up the image, then tucked it into his coat and took to the sky, the disbelief he left behind sucking at him, trying to pull him down.

Gabriel flew high into the clouds, furiously flapping his wings, pumping them until his muscles burned and his lungs screamed. He fought the urge to dive for the ground and tear apart whomever first crossed his path. This world was disgusting to him. Ridiculous. Torturous. He couldn't give a damn about errant princes and spoiled queens. All he wanted was to take what was his and go home.

The following morning, Luck and Gamble ushered Hunter and Storm through another maze of streets, then stopped abruptly beside a magical maintenance wagon. It was little more than a wooden box on wheels, closed on all sides, and with no driver. The side door slid open, and the dwarves hustled them inside.

'What is going on?' said Storm, blinking against the bright overhead light that flicked on as soon as the door closed. The wagon contained nothing at all, not even anything to sit on, so they sat on the uneven wooden floor.

'Where are we going?' asked Hunter, the corners of his eyes creased, his tone laced with concern.

Gamble sucked in a resigned breath. 'We're getting Prince Florian and his godmother, Phinella.'

'Come again?' said Storm.

'Been acting shady,' said Luck.

'Weren't you—only yesterday—extolling the virtues of their match?' said Storm. 'And they've been paired for less than a day. What could they possibly have done in that time?'

Luck scowled. 'Making secret meetings with reporters an' asking questions about the angels.'

'Ah,' said Gamble, as the wagon slowed, 'here we are.'

The lights flicked off as the side door slid open, revealing the Godmother Phinella and Prince Florian. They stood outside a rundown pub—the kind of place Storm would have avoided after dark—and seemed to be having an altercation. Their faces morphed into shock as the dwarves reached out and bundled them inside. The door slid closed in an instant, the wagon taking off without even a jolt as the lights flicked back on.

The wagon's magic smoothed the bumps in the road, but Storm sensed it would be a turbulent ride, at least if Florian and Phinella's furious features were anything to go by.

'Storm?' said Phinella, gaping at Storm. She was a blond-haired, green-eyed whirlwind. Her fairy wings were hidden, but she had an aura that made Storm sit up a little straighter.

Storm was surprised Phinella even knew who she was. 'Hi?' Storm said tentatively. Phinella's mouth twitched, and Storm took the tick to be derisive, so she continued more assertively, 'Sorry about the rough pick up; we wanted to avoid a scene.' She was improvising, but it was probably true.

'Why did you pick us up at all?' said Phinella, casting her eyes over the others.

'Heard you were asking about Rosalind and the fallen,' said Luck, in his usual testy fashion.

Phinella paled.

'What's it to you?' said Florian. He was a typical floppy-haired, chisel-jawed prince, of the type so commonly found in the various kingdoms of Fairy Land. He seemed unusually interested in Storm, his eyes flicking back to her every few moments, although for what reason, Storm couldn't fathom.

'We're trying to stop them,' said Storm. Even if she wasn't totally committed to the idea …

'Hush, girl,' said Gamble. 'We can't trust 'em.'

'Excuse me?' said Phinella. 'You kidnapped us! If anything, you're the untrustworthy ones.'

'S'pose she's got a point,' said Luck.

'What are you trying to stop?' said Florian.

A loaded silence descended, and Storm threw a disbelieving look at Gamble; they were going to have to tell them *something*, otherwise why kidnap them in the first place?

'Urgh, fine,' said Gamble, with an eye roll.

'The fallen angels are destroying Rosalind's lands in the Dark Forest,' said Luck. 'Seem to be mining for something. We don't know what.'

'Won't be good,' Gamble added. 'Knowing Rosalind.'

Phinella seemed to be only half listening, her eyes still on Storm. It was unnerving. And there was something hostile about Phinella's countenance, but Storm couldn't for the life of her work out why. Storm had never even met Phinella.

'We need your help,' said Luck.

'With what?' said Phinella.

'Stopping the angels,' said Storm, because Phinella was *still* looking at her.

Suspicion fell like a blanket across Phinella's features. 'You have proof the angels are destroying the forest?' she said.

'Go an' see for yourself,' Luck said tartly.

'We're being blackmailed,' said Florian, his rushed words shocking everyone into silence.

Storm leaned forward. This whole scenario was becoming more insane by the second. Phinella and Florian had only been paired the previous day …

'Gabriel wants a poisoned apple,' Florian continued. 'We've got three days to get him one.'

The dwarves began to bicker, but the rushing in Storm's ears zoned them out. Gabriel? What did he want with a poisoned apple?

'Hunter,' said Storm, 'we should go … figure out what the angels want.' Because what if the apple was meant for Storm, so the Queen could get rid of her once and for all? And what if Gabriel was a part of that …? Storm repressed the urge to vomit.

'We'll go,' said Phinella. She put an overly familiar hand on Florian's arm, and Storm's gaze glued to the movement, a prickle of interest stirring in her chest. *Surely not.* 'It'll take too long for you to get there,' Phinella added. 'I can transport us in.'

'Transport us all,' said Storm.

'We can't risk you and Florian being together,' said Phinella, her tone short. 'What if they capture you both and force you to marry? It's too dangerous.'

Storm looked blankly at Phinella, and then at Florian, the world going still around her. 'What?' she said, not understanding. Why would anyone force them to marry?

'*The Powers* have decreed you true loves,' said Phinella, doing nothing to hide her bitterness.

Storm couldn't tear her gaze from Florian. *No.* She couldn't marry this … this …

'Which is ridiculous,' said Florian. He put his hand over Phinella's in what could only be described as an intimate gesture.

Storm looked at Hunter before meeting Phinella's gaze once more. 'That's more than ridiculous,' she said. 'No offense, but he's not my true love.'

'Nor are you mine,' said Florian, with a relieved smile.

Phinella's shoulders relaxed, and some of the tension eased.

'But Father and Rosalind are planning our wedding,' said Florian. 'It's to take place in three days.'

'What?' Storm said again, her pulse hammering in her ears.

Hunter took Storm's hand in his. 'We won't let it happen,' he said. 'They can't force the words from your mouths.'

'Do you know why *The Powers*—or Rosalind—would want us to marry?' said Florian.

Storm shook her head. She didn't know her name at this point. Her mind spun, and she couldn't put the pieces together, no matter how she tried. The Queen hated her. Wanted to be rid of her. But marrying her off had never been on the cards. Not once had the Queen mentioned it. For Storm's husband would surely come after the lands and titles that had once been Storm's by right. Why would the Queen expose herself to that risk?

'My stepmother doesn't tell me anything. She thinks I'm a joke ...' Storm paused, still thinking hard, searching for anything that might explain the ludicrous marriage arrangement. 'What about your father?'

'No idea,' said Florian.

'Then we have to find out,' said Storm. 'You're right, we can't go to the forest together.'

'We'll go,' said Phinella, looking up at Florian with a determined nod. 'Tell us exactly where they are.'

Storm barely noticed the ride back to the decaying building the dwarves called *HQ*. Her thoughts raced with unanswered questions: Why would *The Powers* decree her Florian's true love? What did the Queen want? What were the angels looking for in the Dark Forest? Was she just a pawn in their games? And if so, how?

'So Gabriel wants a poisoned apple,' said Genelle, when they were once more seated on the upturned crates.

'Apparently,' said Gamble.

'But Gabriel and the Queen are working together,' said Genelle, 'which means the apple is probably for her.'

'Probably,' said Luck.

'Gabriel must be getting something in return,' said Gamble. 'Question is what?'

'She's already let him destroy her part of the forest,' said Genelle.

'They're fucking,' said Hunter, less composed than Storm had ever seen him. 'Maybe he's fallen in love with her.'

Storm's insides lurched, images of Gabriel and the Queen flooding her mind once more. 'No,' she whispered. 'That can't be it.'

Hunter threw her a questioning look.

'Then what?' said Genelle.

'And why do *The Powers* think you and Florian are true loves?' said Hunter. He set down his tankard with a loud thud.

The dwarves eyed Hunter warily. 'Word on the street is *The Powers* are compromised,' said Genelle.

'If that's true,' said Gamble, 'are *The Powers* working with Rosalind too?'

'Or are the angels calling the shots?' said Genelle.

'But if the angels are callin' the shots, why's Gabriel after a poisoned apple?' said Gamble.

'Well, good luck getting one o' those,' said Luck, 'production locked down as it is.'

'Or maybe the poisoned apple is simply a token of Gabriel's love for Rosalind,' said Hunter, 'and whatever the Queen is up to with *The Powers* has nothing to do with the angels.'

'Nah,' said Luck. 'Too much of a coincidence.'

Storm stood abruptly, almost knocking over her crate. If *The Powers* were compromised, she most likely wasn't Florian's true love. That was good. But if Gabriel and the Queen were truly aligned in their goals, that was bad. Very bad. For the Queen wanted Storm dead.

'Storm?' said Hunter, his features scrunched in concern.

'I'm …' but Storm couldn't find the words to describe what she was. She was not fine. She was confused. She tried to fit the pieces together. Tried to start from the beginning. What were the angels looking for? Why would her marrying Prince Florian help with that? Why did Gabriel want the apple? Her head spun, and she felt suddenly claustrophobic. She had to get out of here. To breathe. To think.

Genelle rolled her eyes. 'You reckon these two can *help* us?' she said to no one in particular. 'Because they seem like a liability to me.'

Storm left the room, heading deeper into the ugly building, pipes and cobwebs the only punctuation against the grey stone.

Prince Florian, the Queen … it wasn't supposed to be like this. And Gabriel …

'Storm?' said Hunter.

Storm jumped as his hand came to rest on her shoulder. She spun and looked up at him.

'Are you okay?' he said. 'Because you don't have to do any of this. You could …'

Storm wrapped her arms around him and hugged him tight. He was warm and homely, and when his muscular arms closed around her, some of the tension melted from her shoulders. They'd been friends for such a long time. He knew the ins and outs of her life in a way none other could, but try as he might, he'd never fully understood.

'I need time to think,' she said into his chest.

'So much is happening at once,' he agreed. 'It's overwhelming.' Silence settled for a beat, then Hunter sucked in a breath, his shoulders suddenly tense. 'You should know I'm all in, Storm. We have to stop the destruction.'

Storm pulled back. Hunter was usually slow and considered about such things, never one to act on impulse, but she nodded, because it made sense; the forests were Hunter's home. She didn't have a home that way …

'I need to be alone,' she said. 'I need to think.'

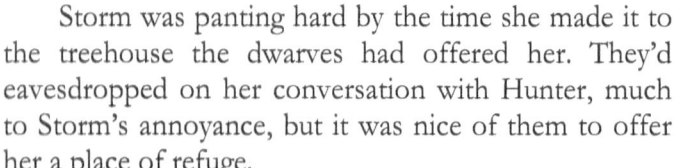

Storm was panting hard by the time she made it to the treehouse the dwarves had offered her. They'd eavesdropped on her conversation with Hunter, much to Storm's annoyance, but it was nice of them to offer her a place of refuge.

It was atop the not-so-dwarf tree she and Hunter had sat under only the day before, and disbelief caught her breath as she took it in; she'd never known the place existed.

It was small and cozy, made from wood hammered together at odd angles, and with a large balcony overlooking the canopy of leaves below. The interior was one big space, housing a seating area, bed, table, and small kitchen, with a separate bathroom at the back.

She retrieved the tin of freshly baked cookies Gamble had told her was in the kitchen cupboard, helped herself to three, then pulled out the magical locket she always wore concealed in her cleavage.

She took a deep, calming breath and then flicked it open, a burst of magic breaking free, shooting up into the air like a silver flare. The shimmering light hung in the sky for a heartbeat, and then faded into the blue, Storm watching until every last trace was gone.

She exhaled, closed the locket, and placed it back beneath the fabric of her dress. Then she sat, waiting for the one person in this world she wanted to see. The only one who would truly care about her strange betrothal to Prince Florian.

She didn't have long to wait, his wings beating gently as he landed with a light thud on the balcony. He strode to the door, his eyes scanning the interior, looking for her, and her heart skipped a beat. They could so rarely be alone together, and just the sight of him made her knees go weak, with his high cheekbones, pointed ears, and intelligent eyes.

'Storm,' he breathed, as his eyes settled on her seated form.

She flew to him, her feet growing wings, and he snatched her up into his arms, pressing his lips to hers with a searing ferocity. She lost all sense of time as he kissed her, engulfed by the sensation, hoping he would never stop.

Her back hit something hard—the wall, she realized—and his movements slowed, becoming tender, savoring every touch. The press of his body against hers lit a fire in her blood, and she moaned into his mouth, her senses overwhelmed by his lips and teeth and tongue.

He slid a hand into her hair as he pulled back, Storm chasing his lips, kissing him one final time before opening her eyes, returning to the world.

His topaz eyes were smoky with lust, and Storm smiled, almost giddy. A smile tugged at his mouth too as he bent to drop another deep kiss on her lips. It set emotions coursing through her she had no words to describe.

'I've missed you,' he said between long, languid kisses, his body still caging her in.

Storm's chest pulsed and her stomach contracted. 'I missed you too,' she said, sliding her hands over the defined ridges of his back, clinging to him, scared they would be forced apart too soon.

He took her hand and led her to the sofa, pulling her onto him so she sat across his lap. He stroked his knuckles down her cheek, then ran his thumb across her lip, watching her as though she might disappear at any moment.

Storm looked away, unable to meet his gaze. '*The Powers* have decreed Florian to be my true love,' she said, hating the tremble in her voice. 'I … they … They're wrong. I love you, Gabriel.'

'And I love you,' he said, without hesitation. He took her hand, then paused, suddenly conflicted. 'But you must go through with the wedding.'

Storm recoiled, snatched her hand away, then scampered to the other side of the sofa, pressing herself back into the arm. He tried to follow, to put their bodies in contact once more. 'No,' she said, holding out her hand to him, and it was as though she'd placed a physical barrier in his way.

He stopped, but did not retreat, watching Storm with desperation in his eyes as she struggled to think, to breathe, to find words to convince him he was wrong. 'Why?' she said eventually, the only word her mind would supply. The only thing that truly mattered.

'*The Powers* are working with the Queen and I,' he said, his eyes tracking her every minute move.

'They're …' *The Queen and I?* Was that how he thought of them? As a pair? Did he … love her? The woman who had treated Storm like a slave? The image of Gabriel sinking his teeth into the Queen's neck flashed before Storm's eyes, and she shuddered.

'They're frauds,' he said, his words snapping Storm back into the moment. Right, *The Powers*. 'They have next to no magic, and are terrified of those who do.'

'But … why?' said Storm, battling the thick treacle that had filled her mind. 'Why must I marry *Florian*?' She spat his name, barely able to say the word. 'Why me?'

Gabriel took a long breath, then the softness in his features disappeared, replaced by something cold and distant. 'The Queen has negotiated a transfer of land as part of your marriage contract.'

Storm sucked in a surprised breath as his words settled, as the pieces slid into place. 'In the Dark Forest?'

Gabriel's gaze became calculating as he studied her. He nodded.

'They said you're destroying it?'

'We are doing what we must,' he snapped. He ran a hand through his hair, then exploded to his feet and turned away. 'The forest is collateral damage, and that is regrettable, but …'

'Why?' she said again, leaning forward. 'Why are you doing it?'

He paced, shoulders stiff, wings flexing in frustration. 'We're searching for a rare mineral,' he said, then came to a stop, facing the wall. 'One we need to restore our homeland to its rightful state; to placate the monsters there. We found traces under the forest, but we need more.'

Storm wrapped her arms around herself, hugging tight. So that's why the angels were here. He had kept her sweet with pretty words and stolen kisses lest she be useful, all the while doing the same to the Queen. He would have no use for either of them once he got what he needed. And what he needed now was for Storm to marry another.

'We must find more,' said Gabriel. He seemed to be speaking to himself as much as Storm.

'So you can leave this place and abandon me? Stuck in a loveless marriage to Prince Florian?'

'No … Storm …' He spun to face her, his features soft, something in his eyes hinting at desolation. He moved towards her, only a pace away, but she held up her hand once more, tears welling behind her eyes.

'I can't do it. Marriage in these lands is … it binds a couple with powerful magic.' Embarrassment flushed hot across Storm's cheeks. Gabriel had been her hope for a better future. How many times had she daydreamed about flying off in his arms to start a new life? But he was as bad as the Queen. Worse, even, for at least the Queen had long since dropped any pretense of liking her. 'I will not marry Florian, for I will never be able to reverse it.'

'You won't need to reverse it,' said Gabriel, his eyes boring into hers with a look she couldn't distinguish. Was it anger, or was it furious passion? Her heart gave a traitorous thud, desperately trying to convince her it was the latter, but she would not be so stupid again. 'We will leave this place together. We will return to my homeland, where Florian cannot follow.'

'Liar,' said Storm. She'd believed him before, but now …

'Storm …' he said, 'please …'

'You will leave me here to my pathetic, lonely life, and you will run back into the arms of whoever awaits in your world.' She laughed, cruelly. 'Can I even travel to your world? I was so caught up in the excitement of you, of the stolen kisses and touches and looks, I never considered the practicalities. How stupid you must think me.'

'Storm,' he said again, pleading. He crossed the space in three quick strides, then dropped to his knees before her. 'We will leave though the House of Portals. I will show you. It was my way here, and will be our way home.'

'*Your* way home, maybe.'

'*Our* way,' he insisted. He took her hands, and she let him, but refused to meet his gaze. 'I love you, Storm. I will not leave this place without you. I came for the mineral, yes, but I came for you too.'

Storm closed her eyes. 'And what does the Queen get?' she said, her words laced with bitterness. 'Did you come for her too?' She didn't let him see her pain, forcing her features into an empty stare.

Gabriel bowed his head for several labored beats. When he looked back into her eyes, he looked … vulnerable. 'How can you say that?' he breathed. 'I do with the Queen what I must for the good of my people, but my guts churn at every contact, every look, and every word. She is as poisoned as the apple she expects me to deliver.'

'That's why she's helping you? So she'll finally have her apple?'

Gabriel nodded.

'You don't care what she intends to do with it?'

'No,' said Gabriel, 'for we will be long gone, back in my world … our world. When I am done with this place, I won't give the Queen a second thought.'

'You'll never find one,' said Storm, seeking words that would hurt him as much as he had hurt her. The Queen had been searching for years, and the dwarves had said production was *locked down*, whatever that meant.

'I'm blackmailing Phinella and Florian,' said Gabriel.

Storm laughed. 'I know.'

Gabriel went still, looking worried for the first time in all the time she'd known him. 'How?'

'They told me. And if you think they're going to help you, you're sorely mistaken.'

Chapter Four

GABRIEL'S SKIN CRAWLED AS he flew for the Dark Forest. He'd come from the Queen's castle, for she'd summoned him, and he couldn't wait to scrub the foul floral stench of her perfume off his skin.

He couldn't hold her off much longer ... it was only a matter of time until he'd have to bed her ... to do things that made him want to stick a knife in his guts. Every time he bit her, or kissed her, it was like sampling rotten fruit, the taste rancid in his mouth.

She insisted on being called *the fairest of them all*, which made her easy to manipulate, but the words snagged in his throat every time.

And then there was Storm, her plain features more beautiful than the Queen could ever hope to be. Feisty to her core, but also delicate and worryingly worn.

He wanted to take Storm and go home to where they belonged, before this strange world pushed her beyond the point of no return.

'How did it go with the Queen?' Michael asked, as Gabriel landed in the Dark Forest.

'Same as ever,' Gabriel snarled.

'The parallels to home are quite striking,' said Michael, his words edged with cruel humor.

Gabriel hurled a rock at him, which he narrowly avoided. Michael laughed. 'Did I touch a nerve, old friend?'

'Have you found any more of the mineral?' said Gabriel, scowling hard.

Michael shook his head. 'You would know if we had.' Michael went quiet for a moment before adding, almost gently, 'And how's the other mission?'

Gabriel shrugged, then punched a tree, his fist leaving a crater in the trunk.

'It'll work out,' said Michael. 'Even if Isaiah has to come in here and drag her kicking and screaming.'

'Isa doesn't have authority here,' said Gabriel, looking around at the trees. Endless fucking trees.

Michael smiled. 'I'm not sure she would see it that way.'

Storm reluctantly climbed down from the treehouse. Gabriel had left shortly after she'd told him his plan was foiled, and she'd spent a few blessed hours in glorious isolation, but she couldn't hide forever. Gabriel had reassured her over and over, saying she was the only one he loved, that he hated the Queen, and that he would take her away from this terrible place.

She wanted to believe him, wanted to kiss this world and its wicked people goodbye, for there was nothing for her here. But she would not give herself away completely. She would defend her heart from him, for she didn't truly know him. How could she? They'd spent so little time together, and yet, she felt as though she'd known him all her life. Like he fitted.

She would help him, would choose to believe he would take her with him when he left, because his promises were the only glimmer of hope she had to hold on to. But she would do so knowing that every word he'd uttered could be a lie.

She would do what she must, but she would not trust him. Even if that meant marrying Florian.

The dwarves and Hunter emerged from the foliage as Storm reached the foot of the tree. She jumped, trying to hide her guilt. How long had they been there? Had they seen Gabriel leave?

'Ah,' said Gamble, 'just in time.'

Storm pushed her trepidation down low and plastered an expectant look on her face. A look that asked, *What next?*

'No time ter dawdle,' said Luck, marching off into the trees. 'We'll miss the Camembert.'

'Come again?' said Storm. But Gamble was already hot on his heels.

They walked awhile, then climbed through a hole between the enormous roots of an ancient walnut tree. Storm didn't bother asking where they were going, for she doubted the dwarves would tell her, and anyway, she was too preoccupied with thoughts of Gabriel to care.

'Here,' said Luck. He handed Storm the dried-out shell of a coconut, liquid sloshing around inside. 'Drink it; it'll help.'

She sniffed it gingerly. The fumes burnt the back of her nose, but it had an alluring sweetness, so she knocked it back in one.

'Oh, my …' said Hunter, his features pinched in concern.

43

'That's the spirit!' said Luck. He downed his own drink, then handed her another.

Storm took a sip as she turned her attention to her surroundings. They'd emerged into a large hall carved from the ground. Tree roots formed the roof, and dappled light filtered through the many holes.

A gaggle of magical creatures crowded around a long banquet table in the middle of the space, dipping rosemary breadsticks into gigantic wheels of melted Camembert, or sipping drinks from coconut halves.

The scene was ludicrous, and yet Storm inched closer to the table as she continued to survey the space. Something about it seemed familiar, although she couldn't work out why; she'd certainly never been here before. Her attention kept wandering back to the roof, and the shafts of light shining through the cracks.

Storm selected a breadstick and dipped it into the gooey cheese, the garlic they'd spiked into the middle of the rounds wafting temptingly up her nose. Hunter was helping himself at the other end of the table, talking to Genelle in animated fashion. He seemed at home with these people—whoever these people were—and Storm was glad, for he would need friends when she left with the angels. If it wasn't all a lie …

Storm bit down, the soft, creamy cheese and crunchy breadstick a taste and texture sensation, but her lips still tingled with the feel of Gabriel's kisses, her skin carrying the memory of his fingers pressing into her hips and waist and …

'It's not that simple,' whispered a sharp male voice behind her.

The tense tone chased her daydream away, but Storm knew better than to turn and look. Instead, she strained to hear every syllable.

'It's fine,' slurred Luck, the alcohol having apparently gone to his head already. 'Iz locked down.'

'Until someone decides to unlock it,' said the man, his tone bordering on anger.

'Who would?' said Luck. 'Who even knows where it is?'

'You told me yourself, you had a close call only recently ...'

'Who is that?' said Hunter, bumping Storm's arm.

Storm jumped, and Hunter chuckled.

'Sorry,' he said. 'Didn't mean to startle you.'

Storm finally allowed herself to look at the man talking to Luck, and found a tall, spindly elf. The elf had short, raven black hair and skin so light it was almost translucent. It was an unusual combination, and it made his green eyes seem positively otherworldly.

'I don't know,' said Storm, 'but he and Luck aren't seeing eye to eye.'

Hunter openly studied the elf, who suddenly turned towards them. The elf's eyes met Hunter's, and their gazes held for a beat, two, three, before the elf finally broke eye contact and stormed away. Luck's eyes narrowed, as though he were trying to solve a tricky equation, his gaze flicking from Storm to Hunter and back again.

'What was that?' Storm asked Hunter, in a low, suggestive tone.

'I ... uh ...'

'You like him!' Storm whispered, nudging Hunter in the ribs.

'Sush,' said Hunter. 'I ...' He faltered, then collected himself. 'What were they arguing about?'

'Don't change the subject.'

'Storm,' said Hunter, his voice stern.

Storm rolled her eyes. 'Poisoned apples, if I had to guess. The elf seemed worried ... something about a recent close call.'

Hunter's brow furrowed. 'Interesting ...'

'Alarming,' said Storm. Although it was good news for Gabriel, she supposed.

Storm didn't sleep a wink that night, endless thoughts warring for space in her mind. Thoughts of how she was betraying Hunter—her only true friend— by helping the angels destroy the Dark Forest. Then of the Queen, the apple, Prince Florian, Gabriel ... Were he and Rosalind laughing at her even now?

The party hadn't lasted long after Luck's altercation with the elf. The gathering was of an unlikely band of creatures who'd come together to deal with the angelic threat. They were unhappy bedfellows, and after Genelle dressed them all down, calling them petty and small-minded, no one had been much in the mood for a party.

The cracks were glaring. Genelle, in her own misguided way, was doing everything she could to keep the group focused, but it wasn't working; another factor in Gabriel's favor ...

Storm was finally drifting off, sometime around dawn, when the dwarves clattered into her room and hauled her out of her narrow, uncomfortable bed.

Across the room, Hunter's bed was still empty. He'd disappeared during the party, saying he was going to find out more about the elf, and hadn't returned ...

Storm barely had time to pull on clothes before the dwarves hurried her out into the street. Unlike Storm, they didn't blink when they found Hunter sitting on the doorstep. His features were neutral, as though there was nothing in the least bit odd about his sitting out here, waiting for someone to let him in.

Hunter rolled to his feet, then Gamble frog-marched them towards the forest, and Storm tugged on Hunter's sleeve, pulling him close. 'What happened?' she whispered conspiratorially.

Hunter shrugged her off. 'Nothing,' he said, his tone almost … hostile. That was strange.

'Hunter …' she said. But he was already striding away, and Storm had to hurry to keep up.

Gamble didn't slow until they were climbing the ladder to the treehouse, the dwarves—in characteristic fashion—offering no explanations.

Storm was dying to know what had happened between Hunter and the elf. Where had he slept? And why was he in such a bad mood? Maybe he'd open up later. Maybe he just needed time … or breakfast …

'It's all right … only us,' Gamble called as she approached the balcony at the top of the ladder.

Storm was the last of their group to reach the top, and she couldn't help but smile when the flustered faces of Phinella and Florian came into view. They'd obviously slept on the balcony after their investigations the previous day, Phinella's cheeks stained a guilty shade of pink.

'I'll put the kettle on,' said Gamble, seemingly oblivious to the scene.

'Biscuits,' said Luck.

The others followed them inside.

'How did you know we were here?' said Phinella, doing her best to smooth her bed hair.

'Who d'you think owns the place?' said Luck.

The kettle whistled, and moments later, they arranged themselves at the rickety table, drinking tea and munching deliciously chocolaty cookies. Not the most nutritious breakfast, but Storm was glad of the sugar.

'You were right,' said Phinella, with little preamble. 'The angels are destroying the Dark Forest.'

'No,' said Luck, deadpan, and Gamble swatted his arm.

'Rosalind wants us to marry,' Florian said to Storm, 'so my father will transfer a chunk of his land in the forest to her. The angels' mining operation has reached the boundary of Rosalind's land, and they can't go any further until an adjacent landowner allows it.'

Storm dredged up every ounce of acting ability she possessed to seem shocked at the news.

'The King still wants the marriage to go ahead,' said Phinella, bunching her fists. 'He still believes in *The Powers.*'

'But we're obviously not going to let that happen,' said Florian, before selecting another biscuit.

Storm took in Florian's easy lean against the back of his chair. He wasn't worried one jot, as was the way of the privileged. Nothing had ever not turned out the way he wanted it to, so he assumed this situation was no different. Storm hoped for her own sake he was right.

'But Gabriel's blackmail still stands,' Phinella said to Florian, her features strained.

'You never told us what he's using to blackmail you?' said Hunter, seemingly in a better mood already. 'We might be able to help.'

Phinella's face blazed. 'He has a picture of us,' she said, lifting her head high and meeting their eyes, despite her obvious discomfort. 'Of Flori and I. An intimate picture that he will send to the press unless we get him an apple.'

'Which we're obviously not going to do,' said Florian, 'but we need to lay low for a while.'

'Because of the picture?' said Storm.

Florian nodded. 'It'll cause a media frenzy, and father …'

'We can't think of a way to stop it,' said Phinella. 'We'd never give Gabriel and Rosalind a poisoned apple—even if we could get our hands on one—but we don't have any other bargaining chips.'

'So we're going to get ahead of it … control the narrative,' said Florian.

Relief flooded Storm, for this meant her marriage to Florian was firmly off the table. She wouldn't even have to lie to Gabriel, for there was nothing she could do. Knowledge of his sordid picture of Florian and Phinella would soon be all over the press, and even better, it was Gabriel's own doing.

'You can borrow my lodge,' said Hunter. 'It's deep in the Enchanted Forest … nobody would find you there.'

'Thank you,' said Phinella.

'And at least the angels can't do more damage to the forest for now,' said Hunter.

Florian nodded. 'Dad won't transfer the land without the marriage, but Gabriel will fight for what he wants.'

Even if it meant sacrificing Storm to a fake marriage …

'Although he can't take the land by force,' said Phinella, 'given the magical protections.'

'He'll try alliances with other landowners,' said Luck.

'The resistance'll look into it,' said Gamble.

They finished their tea, Phinella transported herself and Florian away, and then Hunter jumped to his feet. 'This is it,' he said, pacing. 'How we stop the destruction!'

'Yeh,' said Luck, leaning forward, more animated than Storm had ever seen him. 'We'll get ahead of the angels' next move.'

Storm's heart thundered in her chest. She was glad the threat of marrying Florian was over, but if the angels couldn't get what they needed, they'd have to stay longer, and *she* had no escape. 'What would you do?' said Storm. 'If you were them?'

'Like I said, find the other landowners,' said Luck.

'Who are the other landowners?' said Storm.

'Damned if I know,' said Luck, banging his fist on the table.

'*The Powers'll* know,' said Gamble. 'They keep the records.'

'But they're working with the Queen,' said Hunter. 'They'll be suspicious if we ask them for them.'

'I'll go,' said Storm.

The others turned confused eyes upon her. 'They're working with the Queen,' Luck said slowly, treating her like a child.

'Yes, thank you,' said Storm, testily. 'I am aware. But there's no hope of my marrying Florian now; not after the story of his affair breaks. I'll pretend I'm heartbroken, that I'm desperate for a true love as eligible as he …'

'One who owns a section of the prestigious Dark Forest?' said Gamble, catching on.

'Exactly.'

'But they're in the Queen's pocket,' said Hunter. 'It's not like they'll let you marry against her wishes.'

'We don't know that,' said Storm. 'Maybe Rosalind's deal with *The Powers* was a one-time thing. Maybe they hate her too …'

'It's too dangerous,' said Hunter.

'There's no other way,' said Storm. 'And if we don't try something, and the angels get their hands on the forest ...'

Hunter growled in frustration.

'Not the finest plan I've ever heard,' said Gamble, watching Storm carefully.

'But it's the only one we have,' said Luck.

And the only way Storm could think of getting a message to Gabriel. It was too risky to ask for more time alone, and she had to warn him about the resistance ... to help.

Chapter Five

THE FOLLOWING DAY, STORM snuck through the back entrance of the building *The Powers That Be* called home. Out the front, a mob of reporters waited, along with a sea of spectators, all salivating over the prospect of additional details about the breaking story that Prince Florian and his godmother were a couple.

They were demanding to know how this could have happened. Were *The Powers* losing their touch? There had been rumors of a royal wedding … had this been the plan all along?

It was easy to slip past them, preoccupied as they were, and Storm pushed through the almost hidden staff entrance with not a glance in her direction. The problem was, once she was inside, she had no idea where to go.

She'd never been inside the elaborate building, and the dwarves had been of little help, so she had no choice but to scout around and hope for the best. Maybe she would come across a member of staff who would take pity on her …

But the place was like a ghost town. She didn't see another soul as she walked along the marble-tiled halls. The walls of the staff corridor were bland, painted a terrible yellow color, the doors a dark, varnished wood.

She cracked the door at the end and peered through. It led to a short set of steps covered in plush red carpet, the walls adorned with gilt-framed landscapes, but still no sign of life.

She stepped through and headed to her left, which seemed to lead deeper into the building. Her feet were silent on the thick carpet, and she strained to pick up any sounds. Nothing.

She was doing a terrible job of protecting her heart from Gabriel. She'd resolved not to trust him, and yet the minute their escape was threatened, she'd put herself in harm's way to help him. She had it bad, and all she could do was hope against hope his words were true, for she didn't know how she would recover if it was all a lie. How could anyone come back from that kind of betrayal?

She reached the far end of the wide, column-lined corridor and descended two shallow steps to the closed double doors. They seemed like doors to somewhere important, and she pressed her ear to the wood, listening intently.

Again, nothing.

She took a deep breath, her pulse spiking as she realized she had little choice but to go through, with absolutely no knowledge of what awaited the far side. But just as she reached for the handle, both doors swung inward with a whoosh of air, and Gabriel's divine form stared back at her, surprise taking hold of his face.

'Storm,' he said curtly, his voice little more than a snap.

'I ...'

Gabriel gave a firm shake of his head, and Storm's eyes flicked past his shoulder. She couldn't see much, given he was at least a head taller than she, and there was the matter of his wings, but the sounds of shuffling told her others were present.

'Show her in,' said a thin male voice.

Gabriel closed his eyes for a beat. 'Thank you for coming,' he said. 'I assume you're here on behalf of the Queen?'

'No,' said Storm. She didn't know what he was playing at, but she was here on a mission, and she would see it through. 'I am here because *The Powers* made a terrible mistake! How could Florian be my true love, when ...' She hid her face in her hand, pretending to be distraught. 'I'm sorry ... it's just so painful.'

Storm stepped past Gabriel into the room and found four old men dressed in red robes sat atop throne-like chairs. She took in every detail her senses could supply: grey hair, crowns resting on their heads, wine goblets in hand.

'I thought we would be married! That he would give me the cutest little royal babies, and that we would live out our days in peace and harmony! And then ...' She choked, as though holding back tears. 'Then, I discovered he is in love with *another.*'

The old men threw exasperated looks to one another, as though they could not believe an emotional woman had made it into their inner sanctum.

'You must put it right,' Storm said indignantly, squaring her shoulders as though incensed. 'You must find my real true love, for I deserve that much, after the way you have toyed with my heart.'

'Your Majesty,' said one, the respectful address taking her by surprise, 'we were just now discussing the very same.'

'You were?' she said, not sure whether to believe him.

'I want someone with land in the Dark Forest,' she said. 'I've planned an adorable getaway home, and it would break my heart not to see my plans through.'

A second of the men gave her a skeptical look. Maybe she was taking it a tad too far ... 'What is *he* doing here?' she said, throwing a disgusted look at Gabriel.

Gabriel lifted one eyebrow, the light of entertainment dancing in his eyes.

'He has offered to help in the quest to find your true love,' said the first man.

'Why?' said Storm, her heart thudding loudly in her ears. She threw Gabriel a questioning look.

'I believe he would like you out of the castle, so he may more easily play house with Queen Rosalind,' said a third man, sadistically.

Storm narrowed her eyes, then shrugged. 'Very well,' she said, 'then I suggest we search for candidates together.'

'That isn't how true love works,' said the fourth man, although his attempt to divert her was a weak one.

'No harm in letting them look,' said the first. He seemed relieved at the prospect of a painless resolution. 'We will consult the magic afterwards, although there's no guarantee any of the landowners in the forest will be your true love.'

'Very well,' said Storm, with a nod. She turned on her heel, Gabriel already ahead of her.

He led them through a maze of corridors, his shoulders rigid, his steps so fast she had to run every few paces to keep up.

'Gabriel,' she said, her voice hushed.

He continued as though he hadn't heard.

'Gabriel,' she said again, louder, her tone bordering on anger.

He spun and glared at her, then shook his head ever so slightly.

Oh. Of course. They were being watched.

He continued, pushing open a door to their right a little further along the corridor. They entered, Gabriel standing back so she could go first, although the move felt less of a considerate gesture, and more like she was a prisoner and he her guard.

'Michael,' said Gabriel, nodding at an angel sitting at a desk near the windows. The windows were set high into the wall, and it made the room feel oppressive, like a cage.

Storm shuddered as she looked around at the walls lined with books, maps, and stacks of scrolls. One map caught her eye, the words *The Dark Forest* scrawled at the top. She stepped closer and studied the untidy lines that split the forest into sections, each one belonging to a different royal house.

'Progress?' snapped Gabriel.

Storm spun to face them, surprised to find Michael's eyes glued to her.

There was something familiar about the male ... 'Have we met before?' she asked, her brain clenching, desperately trying to place him.

Michael's eyes flicked to Gabriel, as though asking for permission to speak.

'Michael is my right hand,' said Gabriel. 'It's possible you've seen him around.'

The answer didn't feel like the whole truth, but Gabriel didn't give her time to dwell. 'Well?' he said. 'Spit it out.'

Michael's lips curled into a smile. Apparently Gabriel didn't scare Michael like he did everyone else ...

'Queen Rosalind's section of the forest has three borders,' said Michael. 'One is owned by Prince Florian's father, one by an adventuring king who was last seen over a decade ago, and one belongs to no one.'

'What?' said Storm. 'How is that possible?'

'The Queen who owned it died, but she didn't name a successor. Three children survived her, each of whom lays claim to the land.'

'So the land's in limbo?' said Storm.

'Exactly,' said Michael. 'None of them owns it, and each refuses to allow ownership to sit with another.'

'Doesn't it just go to the oldest son?' said Storm, her tone scathing.

'With commonplace assets such as palaces, jewels, and titles, yes,' said Michael, 'but ancient magic binds the forest. As the Queen failed to stipulate an heir, all three of the heirs must agree.'

'And if they never come to an agreement?' said Storm.

'Then the issue passes to their children, and their children, and so on, becoming ever more complex as the family tree grows, until someone manages to whip them all into line.'

'Gods,' said Storm.

'That land is our only hope,' said Gabriel. 'Unless you have a lead on the adventuring King?'

Michael snorted. 'If rumors can be believed, he's in the clutches of the sirens of the Great Lagoon. He's alive and kicking, so the land is still very much his, but retrieving him seems … tricky.'

'Then we must convince the three warring heirs to sell their share of the Dark Forest to us,' said Gabriel.

Michael laughed. 'How? They already have riches, and they won't give up the prestige lightly.'

'Then come up with ideas,' Gabriel barked. 'I will update Isaiah, and I'm taking Storm with me.'

Gabriel raced through the corridors and flung open the staff door, not hesitating before sweeping Storm up into his arms and taking to the sky.

Storm threw the hood of her cloak over her head and buried her face in the crook of his neck, lest anyone below—most concerningly, Hunter—realize it was her in Gabriel's hold.

He pulled her close, the warm, spicy scent of him enveloping her, and she inhaled greedily.

When they'd left Via d'Magical behind, Storm lifted her face and looked up at his serious features.

'You could have ruined the whole plan,' he said, although his voice contained as much concern as rebuke.

Storm laughed cruelly. 'What plan? It was your blackmailing Florian and Phinella that caused this shit show. I'm helping clear up *your* mess, so we can get the hell out of here.'

Gabriel's hold tightened, and a zing of awareness raced through her. She traced a finger around his pointed ear, and he growled.

'Storm,' he said, his voice gravelly, 'don't.'

'Why not?' she whispered, doing it again. 'There's no one here to see us.'

'I need to concentrate,' he said, although his thumb skirted her ribs in a way that said he was at least a little game.

Storm placed a featherlight kiss on his neck, and Gabriel's breath hitched, the sound sending a shot of electricity through her. She ran her hand up his muscular back, under where his wings connected to his shoulders, then reached up and pressed a single finger to the top edge of his wing. He shivered.

'Storm,' he choked, 'if you want to die, this is a good way to go about it.'

She huffed a frustrated breath and removed her finger. Instead, she peppered him with questions about Isaiah, and where Gabriel was taking her.

He was disappointingly tight-lipped, but it wasn't long before they swooped down into the trees, landing in a clearing. A beech tree of modest height but significant girth stood before them, and Storm eyed the tree as Gabriel set her on her feet. He offered no explanation as he took her hand, pulling her directly towards the trunk.

'Gabriel,' she stuttered when he showed no signs of slowing. He hit the tree, but instead of ricocheting backwards, he passed straight through. He yanked her behind him, a flash of purple light and the barest of sucking sensations against her skin the only sign anything unusual had occurred.

They emerged into an atrium of sorts, tree roots covering the floor, a column of light shining down from far above, illuminating a strange, twisting, metallic sculpture in the middle of the space. Simple wooden doors led off on four sides, one of which they'd stepped through.

Gabriel tugged Storm towards a spiral staircase that hugged a tree trunk off to their right, but Storm pulled back. Her head hurt, her pulse raced, and a barrage of confusion hit her. 'No,' she said firmly. 'I'm not going anywhere until you tell me where the hell this is!'

Gabriel rounded on her, his big, powerful frame crowding her, but if he meant to intimidate, he missed his mark, for his eyes gleamed with longing. 'Storm,' he said, censoringly.

'Gabriel,' she replied, in a matching tone.

He leaned in so his lips brushed her ear, and her pulse spiked. 'This is the House of Portals. I will tell you everything when we are *safely* upstairs.'

The way he said the word *safely* was what made her buckle, as though they were in serious danger where they stood. Her pulse hammered harder as fear coursed through her blood.

Storm took a breath. 'Fine,' she said, allowing him to lead her to the staircase. Storm went first, but Gabriel was only inches behind, so close she could feel his body heat.

He snatched up her hand as soon as they emerged at the top, and a thrill skittered up her spine. His protective fingers entwined with hers, the sensation so distracting she almost didn't realize they'd stopped before a hatch in the tree trunk. He rapped on the wood, and the hatch slid sideways to reveal a pixie peering out from behind a counter on the other side.

Gabriel ran his thumb down Storm's palm, and her breath caught in her throat, then a bolt of pain hit behind her eyes. She scrunched her eyes shut as Gabriel said, 'I require the use of a speaking portal.' The pain receded just in time for her to see him slide something across the counter, although she couldn't make out what.

'The usual?' said the pixie, in a flirtatious tone, her eyes sparkling.

Storm gripped Gabriel's hand harder, and a smile pulled at the corner of his lips. 'Yes,' he said.

The pixie handed over a large, ornate key with a red tassel swinging from the end, and then the hatch snapped shut.

'This way,' said Gabriel.

They climbed higher up the staircase, until they came out onto a circular balcony where ladders, narrow wooden steps, spiral staircases, rope bridges, and cargo nets led off in all directions. Some went higher, some travelled down the trunks of neighboring trees, and others continued on the same level, joining one tree to the next.

Storm's feet rooted to the spot, her mind struggling to understand what her eyes were showing her. 'I thought we came into a tree ...' said Storm. 'What is this place?'

Gabriel cast about with wary eyes, as though worried who might be listening. 'This is the House of Portals,' he said, his voice a gruff whisper. 'The tree we came through was a hole from your world to here, nothing more, and there are thousands more like it ... portals to every discoverable world.'

Storm's mind whirred as she tried to process his words. 'I could go anywhere?' she said, tempted to climb the nearest ladder and see where it would take her.

Gabriel's grip tightened. 'Many have lost their way wandering worlds,' he said. 'It is a tricky business, navigating, remembering who you are and where you are from.'

'We could wander worlds forever,' said Storm, excitement unfolding in her chest. 'Just you and me together, no one to stop us.'

Gabriel stepped close, barely a sliver of air remaining between them. 'You're coming back to my world,' he growled, 'with me.'

His eyes bored into hers, and the conviction she saw there painted a smile across her lips. 'Okay,' she said with a shrug, because with his beautiful topaz eyes, he could probably convince her to do almost anything.

'And wandering worlds is not the romantic escape you imagine,' he said, pulling her towards another spiral staircase.

'Why not?' she said, the rickety metal steps clunking under their feet.

'Because the worlds know you don't belong. Unless one takes a liking to you, they will work against you at every turn.'

Storm's mind exploded with questions, but she didn't have time to ask them, because Gabriel had once again halted. He stuck the key into a hole in the tree trunk and turned it, causing a section of bark to swing forward.

He pulled her through the opening, and the door closed behind them, enclosing them in a room that looked like the home of a woodpecker, nothing adorning the curved wooden walls.

In the middle of the space was a swirling black hole, not quite big enough for a person to fit through. Storm approached it, but Gabriel pulled her back, wrapping his arm around her waist to hold her in place.

'Isaiah,' he called.

'Yes?' said a woman's voice, floating through the black.

They exchanged no pleasantries. Gabriel updated the woman with swift, precise words, and then silence settled. Storm tried to pull away, assuming the woman had gone, about to make a start on her long string of questions, but Gabriel gripped her tightly.

'She is there?' said the voice.

'Yes,' said Gabriel.

'You wish to bring her now?' The tone was derisive, as though his suggestion displayed weakness.

'Yes,' Gabriel said again.

Storm's heart leapt into her mouth as she realized what they meant … the implications of that simple little word. *Now?*

'No,' said Isaiah, her tone firm and cold. 'Finish your mission.'

A strange mix of relief and disappointment welled in Storm's chest.

'Why?' Gabriel said through gritted teeth.

'For the children,' said the woman, 'as you well know.'

<hr />

After several perilous staircases and two visits to hatches in the trees—one to return the key with the red tassel, and a second to retrieve a new, smaller, sleeker one—Gabriel pushed open another bark door.

Storm stepped through, surprised to find a large but simple bedroom that wouldn't have looked out of place in Rosalind's castle. The bed was big enough for at least three, which Storm supposed was to cater for the variety of creatures that must use the portals. Storm perched upon it, the only place to sit, other than the window seats.

Gabriel's shoulders seemed finally to relax as the door clicked shut. He turned the key in the lock, then paced the length of the room, his brow furrowed, lost in thought.

Storm watched and waited, taking in the flex of his wings every time he changed direction, and the way his forearms danced as he clenched and unclenched his fists.

'I shouldn't have brought you here,' he said eventually, his voice gravelly. 'I've put you in danger, and for that, I'm sorry.'

Storm laughed. 'You know I live with the constant threat of death, right? The Queen wants nothing more than to rid herself of me ... has tried many times ... it's probably the reason she wants that apple.'

He stopped pacing and faced her. 'This is different,' he said. 'It's …'

Storm waited for him to finish, but the words never came; he could be like this when things got serious. It was strange, how she knew those kinds of details, yet she couldn't even remember how they'd first met. Some magnetism pulled them together whenever they were close, but …

'The apple wouldn't kill you,' he said.

Storm tilted her head to one side and fixed him with a questioning look.

He ran a frustrated hand through his hair. 'I made her tell me what it's for.'

Storm sat up straighter. 'And?'

'The poison causes an eternal slumber, not death.'

Storm considered his words. 'I'm not sure an eternal slumber is much different …'

'The cure is true love's kiss,' he said, although he seemed embarrassed to utter the words.

'You don't believe in true love?' said Storm, furrowing her brow. Fairy Land thrived on its existence, amplified by *The Powers,* the media, and the royal houses at every opportunity. It was almost a currency.

'No,' said Gabriel. 'My heart chooses who to love, and that is all that matters.'

Their eyes met, and silence stretched between them. They were finally alone, without the threat of interruption or exposure. The realization sent elation bubbling through Storm's chest, for there were things she needed to know.

'What did Isaiah mean, when she told you to complete your mission?' she asked.

'You know,' he said, with a frown.

'To find some mineral in the Dark Forest, mine it, and take it home?'

'Yes. It's important …'

'If it's so important, then why do you want to leave?'

He stilled. 'Because you're more important.'

'More important than saving your homeland?' she scoffed.

He shook his head. 'It's not straightforward.'

Storm balled her fists into the fabric of the duvet, then stood and paced to the window. She took a long breath, forcing calm through her veins as she watched the branches blowing in the breeze beyond the glass. 'I don't understand.'

'You will,' he said, coming up behind her. He placed his hands on her shoulders, then slid them down her arms, all the way to her fingertips.

Storm tried to focus, but the blood rushed from her brain, following his touch.

'Who was the woman?' said Storm. Her eyes fluttered closed as Gabriel's fingers traced the hollow of her waist.

'My leader,' he said, 'and she's caused me more pain than I care to recall.'

'How?' She turned to face him, and a pulse of red-hot anger stabbed through her, along with another searing pain in her head.

Storm winced, and Gabriel's face screwed up with concern.

'I'm fine,' she said, sucking in a breath, forcing the pain away.

Gabriel cupped her face in his hands, examining her. When he found nothing to concern him further, he kissed her, and Storm let the firm press of his lips chase away her curiosity. But then he pulled back. 'Michael just set off a flare,' he said, his voice husky and regretful. He rested his forehead against hers, and she savored the sensation.

'That means we have to go?'

He nodded.

It was probably for the best, for the others must surely be wondering where she was … would be suspicious when she returned.

Gabriel pressed another kiss to her lips. 'We're going to get the hell out of Fairy Land,' he said, 'and when we do, I promise you'll understand.'

Storm fired question after question at Gabriel as they returned to *The Powers That Be*. Why did Gabriel's homeland need the mineral he was mining? What had his leader meant about *the children*? What if his world rejected Storm? He'd said that could happen when people hopped between worlds, so how would she fit into his? Would she also have to answer to his leader? Would she be swapping one cage for another?

Gabriel refused to give anything away, and by the time they reached Michael in the record room, Storm's blood boiled.

Michael's features turned wary the moment they entered, apparently picking up the tension with little trouble. 'Everything okay?' he said, his eyes flicking from Gabriel to Storm and back again.

'Fine,' said Gabriel, at the same moment as Storm said, 'Peachy.'

'Seems like it …' said Michael.

'You sent a flare?' Gabriel snapped.

'I've found a way,' said Michael.

'To get the land from the kids of the dead Queen?' said Storm.

Michael nodded.

'How?' said Gabriel.

'A covenant set into the magic.'

'Go on,' said Gabriel.

'We transfer the land into the name of an eligible royal, and simply take it from under their noses,' said Michael. 'If they don't notice within three days, the land is ours for good.'

'Using me as your eligible royal?' said Storm, folding her arms. 'I'm not sure I still qualify.'

'You do,' said Michael. 'I checked.'

'So we just … steal it? That's legal?' said Storm.

'This land is strange,' said Gabriel.

'It's brilliant, actually,' said Storm. 'If the potential heirs are too busy fighting among themselves to monitor what's going on with the forest, they don't deserve to inherit.'

'It's even better than that,' said Michael. 'During those three days, Storm may act as though she owns the land.'

'We can mine,' said Gabriel.

'Yes,' said Michael. 'Although if anyone notices, they may use force to stop her.'

'And by that, you mean?' said Storm.

'Anyone may kill you during the three-day window, and to do so would break no laws. If they succeed, their claim supersedes yours, and they must only wait the duration of time you have remaining before claiming the forest as their own.'

'Great,' said Storm. 'More people wanting to kill me … just what I need.'

'We'll keep you safe,' said Gabriel.

'How?' said Storm.

'We'll hide you,' said Gabriel.

'That will do nothing but attract attention,' said Storm. 'I should go back to the resistance and pretend I found nothing here … try to divert them.'

'I can't protect you there,' said Gabriel, his eyes hard.

'If I don't return, they'll come after me. Unless … I could hide in the House of Portals? No one would find me there …'

'No,' said Michael. 'The House is not a place of refuge.'

'We'll pretend we kidnapped you,' said Gabriel.

'Then Rosalind will come for me,' said Storm, 'and will turf you out of her land in the forest.'

'We don't need her land any longer,' said Gabriel.

'She'll know you're up to something. She's relentless and resourceful, and will rejoice that my claiming this land will give her a legitimate reason to kill me.' Storm inhaled deeply. 'The only option is for me to return to the resistance and do what I can to keep them off the scent. It's only three days …'

Gabriel scowled, his wings pulsing. 'Fine,' he said. 'I don't like it, but I suppose you're right.'

Storm shook her head in annoyance, her eyes wide, then turned to Michael. 'What do you need me to do?'

'The moment you sign here, the countdown begins.'

Storm took the quill Michael offered, and held her breath as she scribbled her name.

Chapter Six

'WELL?' SAID LUCK, AS Storm stepped through the door to the treehouse.

He seemed agitated, and Storm supposed they were anxious for news … she'd been gone a while.

'I didn't find out much, I'm afraid,' said Storm, taking a seat at the table. '*The Powers* are preoccupied with Phinella and Florian. They made me wait half the day before they would see me, and when they finally let me in, they had little sympathy.'

'You found nothing?' said Luck.

Storm dropped her head to look at her hands, hoping they didn't see straight through her. 'The Queen's land in the Dark Forest borders land belonging to a king who's been missing for a decade. He's an adventurer. If we could track him down, maybe he would help us, but it's not much to go on … I'm sorry.'

'Unless the angels get ter him first,' said Luck, banging his fist on the table.

'We'll put out feelers,' said Gamble, although, unusually, she didn't bother to chastise Luck for his tone. She was disappointed too, then.

'We'll regroup tomorrow,' said Luck. He pushed to his feet and headed for the ladder, and Gamble followed behind.

When he and Gamble had disappeared through the hole in the balcony floor, Hunter fixed Storm with a stern look. Gone was the usual softness about his eyes, no sign of his easy smile, and the transition made Storm shiver.

'What?' she said, trying to sound natural, although she was certain she hadn't succeeded.

'You know what,' he said. 'You just lied through your teeth! You can fool them, but I know you better.'

'Hunter ...' Storm looked away, trying to slow things down, to give herself time to think.

'Don't *Hunter* me,' he said, his voice colder than she'd ever heard it.

She frowned in confusion. 'Did something happen while I was away?'

'Yes, something happened: you did a deal with the angels. With *Gabriel.*'

'What are you talking about?' said Storm, but she could feel the flush of red fanning out across her face, betraying her.

'I saw Gabriel fly into this very treehouse when you said you needed time alone. And then, earlier today, I saw you fly along Via d'Magical in Gabriel's arms. You didn't seem unhappy about it.'

Of course he'd been watching. He was a hunter, hated the angels, and cared for her. He was diligent, and had nothing else to occupy his time. 'Hunter ...' she said again, this time in defeat. 'I ... had no choice.'

'You love him?' he accused, his eyes watching her like a hawk.

She inhaled deeply as she considered his question. 'I'm not sure I even trust him, but I can't keep living the life I have here, working as Rosalind's slave, always looking over my shoulder in case she's finally found a way to break the magic that protects me.'

'You're the rightful heir of half of what she holds dear,' said Hunter. 'You could fight back.'

'No,' said Storm. 'The Queen is the rightful owner. She tricked me, yes, but it is hers, fair and square. I gave it to her on a platter ...'

'That's not true,' Hunter insisted, but Storm couldn't even recall the details now; it was too long ago to dredge to the surface.

'She coerced you. Lied to you. It wasn't fair!'

Storm shrugged. 'All is fair in love and war ... isn't that how the saying goes?'

'So, what?' said Hunter. 'You'll fly off into the sunset with Gabriel?'

Storm scoffed. 'It's hardly like that.'

'It's exactly like that.'

'The angels don't even want to be here, and the sooner they find what they're looking for, the sooner everyone gets what they want.'

'But at what price?' said Hunter. 'The price of the forest?'

Storm faltered. 'The forest will recover,' she said, although her words were tentative. 'They don't want to cause damage, but it's the only way for them to find what they need ... to save their homeland.'

'You've bought their little story hook, line, and sinker,' he said, with a harsh laugh.

'What other explanation is there?'

'That they're here to destroy our world and steal our wealth, then move onto another and do the same.'

'No,' said Storm, adamantly. She'd been unsure before, but not after today. She'd heard their leader through the portal, had seen the look on Gabriel's face. 'They just want to go home.'

'And you'll go with them?'

'Yes,' said Storm, never surer of anything. 'You're all I have here, and you'll be fine without me. You have the forests, and now the resistance …'

Hunter shook his head, the movement slow and calculating. 'My life will be a husk without you, but you've made up your mind, so I won't try to convince you. You've already chosen the angels over me and all the possibilities for your life here.'

'Hunter, it's not like that …'

Hunter pulled back his shoulders, his features a mask of indifference. 'And if you want me to keep your secret, there's something you must do for me.'

Storm's stomach sank and her mouth dropped open, and it occurred to her that maybe she didn't really know Hunter at all.

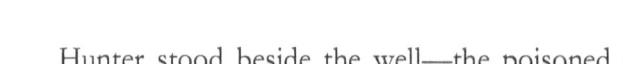

Hunter stood beside the well—the poisoned well Luck had warned them not to touch—and Storm's eyes went wide. 'You can't be serious,' she said. She took a tentative step forward, but the memory of Luck's vehemence made her wary.

'I can be serious,' said Hunter, who was casting around, looking for something.

'What are you doing?' said Storm. 'Why …?' But then she realized, and the thought pulled her up short. This well was the close call. The tunnel had been almost impossible to find again, even for Hunter, who knew every bush craft secret in the trade.

Was that the real reason Hunter had pursued the elf after the party? To find out more? Was he ruthless and calculating when she'd thought him sweet and kind? But then, could a person not be both under the right circumstances?

'What will you do with a poisoned apple?' said Storm.

Hunter checked, faltering for a moment, but then continued without a word, tracing the roots that came down through the ceiling.

'Hunter, I don't understand ...' Although maybe that was because her mind was sluggish. He'd pulled her out of bed long before sunrise.

'You will,' he said. He stuck a root through a hole in the well's brickwork, threading it through until the end rested in the water.

'So, what?' said Storm. 'Now poisoned apples will grow on the tree above?'

Hunter shrugged. 'I guess we'll find out.'

'What if someone gets there first?' said Storm, making to follow him out of the tunnel. 'A child? Or an animal? Or ... anyone? Or a member of the resistance? There'll be hell to pay if they find out ...' And Storm needed the resistance to trust her.

Hunter whirled around. 'You're staying here,' he said, without a hint of concern. 'Listen for me above. When I say the word, remove the roots from the well, and for Gods' sake, don't get any water on your hands.'

Storm threw up her arms, then took a seat on a rock near the well. Because what other choice did she have?

She didn't have long to wait before she heard something above. She went as still as a statue, her pulse pumping in her ears as she strained to listen. She could make out not one voice, but two, their words muted by the soil and roots, but both were female.

Dread clawed at Storm's insides as she listened, and from what she could make out, they were arguing.

'If you don't tell him, I will,' said one of the women.

'I will … I promise.'

'You've broken too many promises … I don't believe you anymore.'

'I'll tell him. I will. It's just …'

'Just what?'

'You know it's complicated.'

'Ladies,' said a kindly male voice—Hunter, 'I beg your pardon, but you're scaring away the game.'

'Can't you see we're in the middle of something?'

'Any chance you could be in the middle of something somewhere else?' he said.

Storm could sense the strain in Hunter's voice, even through the filter of the ground.

'Urgh, men!' one of them shouted, and then, silence.

'Storm, pull the roots out,' said Hunter, his tone urgent. 'Pull them out now!'

Storm pulled the roots free of the water as quickly as she could, careful not to spray any droplets, and to keep her hands away from the damp sections.

As soon as she was done, she snatched up the glow stone Hunter had placed near the well and ran for the tunnel, her heart thundering as she traversed the uneven ground. She was so caught up in her own thoughts, she almost missed the voices coming towards her, low and serious.

'Quickly now,' said a male voice. 'We haven't much time.'

Storm extinguished the stone as she ducked into a side tunnel with only moments to spare, slowing her pace to ensure she made no sound. She worked hard to control her ragged breathing, concentrating so hard she almost forgot to notice who passed by.

She strained to see their faces in the near-dark, their glow stone set low, giving off only the dimmest of light. But she recognized the tall, slight form, dark hair, and pointed ears: the elf from the Camembert party. And in the shadows on the other side ... *Goddess,* it was Hunter.

———

Storm slipped out of the tunnel onto Via d'Magical, taking care to draw as little attention as she could. She was considering the pros and cons of sending Gabriel a flare when Gamble and Luck appeared by her side.

'What you up to?' said Luck, narrowing his eyes suspiciously.

'I needed to get out of the treehouse,' said Storm. 'I think better when I walk.'

'What you thinking about?' said Luck.

Gamble elbowed him. 'Where's Hunter?' she said. 'We have news.'

'An' only want ter say it once,' said Luck.

Storm rolled her eyes. 'Hunter went for a walk too; I don't know where. Neither of us is used to being around other people so much of the time, and it's ... uncomfortable.'

'Sorry for the inconvenience, Princess,' said Luck. 'Not like there's a troop of fallen angels ripping apart our land or anything ...'

Was that why he was in such a foul mood, or had something happened?

'Come along,' said Gamble. She linked her arm through Luck's, and tugged him up the street. 'We'll wait for Hunter at the treehouse.'

They clambered to the top of the dwarf tree and found Hunter already waiting. Storm's eyes bored into his, showing him just how angry she was. He'd set her up; that was the only logical explanation. But had it worked? Did he have an apple?

Storm had no need of the thing, but she was beyond curious to know why Hunter wanted one badly enough to take such a risk. Not to mention, she wanted to know more about the elf. Did he want an apple? And if so, was Hunter working with him, or against him?

'What's going on with you two?' said Luck, interrupting their staring contest.

'Nothing,' said Storm, snapping her gaze away. 'What did you want to tell us?'

Luck furrowed his brow as his eyes flicked between Hunter and Storm. 'You pissed he spent the night with our elf friend?'

Storm scowled. 'No.'

'Luck, knock it off,' said Gamble. 'We have more important matters to discuss.'

Luck rolled his eyes. 'We've turned over every stone we can find, yet have no leads on the missing King,' said Luck.

'That explains your mood, then,' said Storm.

Luck's scowl morphed into a sneer.

'We're looking into other owners,' said Gamble, 'so all hope is not lost, an' we're getting reports of angelic activity on the eastern border. It's unclear if they've crossed over, but something must be going on with the landowner there.'

Storm's stomach dropped. *Shit*. She still had two days before that land was legally hers, which meant another two days of danger. What if they already knew? Was that why Luck was watching her with such hostility? Storm's stomach roiled and she worried she might be sick. Why couldn't her life just be simple?

'But *The Powers* ain't playing ball,' said Luck. 'Good for nothing frauds. Not a lick of magic between them, an' when we face a threat to our world, what do they do? Nothing, that's what.'

'We're exploring other options,' said Gamble, reassuringly. 'We'll find a way.'

Luck scowled again, then rummaged in the back of a cupboard and pulled out a bottle of amber colored liquid. He headed for the balcony.

Gamble shook her head. 'Long time since I've seen him like this. Best give him some space,' she said, then patted each of them in maternal fashion and headed after Luck.

'What the fuck are you playing at?' Storm hissed, as soon as the dwarves were out of earshot.

'What do you mean?' said Hunter, his tone casual and unconcerned.

'Don't play dumb with me. I saw you and the elf in the tunnels. You tried to set me up!'

'Don't be dramatic.'

'Oh, I'm sorry. How would you like me to react after finding out I have no freaking idea who you are? That you would sell me down the river at your earliest convenience?'

'Bit rich coming from you,' said Hunter. He leaned against the table, crossing his feet at the ankles.

'That's *different*.' *Sort of.* 'Well? Did you get one?'

Hunter smiled his adorable lopsided grin. The one that made people do things for him because he looked dim-witted yet well-meaning. 'Wouldn't you like to know,' he said.

Chapter Seven

THE DWARVES STAYED IN the treehouse on account of Luck being too drunk to safely climb down the ladder, so Storm had no further opportunity to probe Hunter about the apple. She surreptitiously searched for any sign, looking for bulges in his pockets, following the direction of his gaze when he thought no one was looking, sitting close to his possessions to see if it made him nervous. It didn't. He gave absolutely nothing away. Damn him.

Storm slept badly. The dwarves took the bed, Hunter rustled up a hammock from somewhere, which he strung between two branches over the balcony, meaning Storm had little choice but to sleep on cushions on the floor, the sofa not long enough even for her. So when Florian and Phinella appeared without so much as a puff of smoke early the following morning, Storm was both glad of the distraction, and ready to bite someone's head off. Although, maybe her lack of sleep was secondary to her fear of discovery ...

'What are you doing here?' said Storm, managing to keep her tone light. 'I thought you were enjoying your forest hideaway?'

'We were,' said Florian, dropping an arm around Phinella's shoulders, 'but Gamble asked for a favor.'

Gamble jumped out of bed, her long white nightdress wafting around her legs. 'Well?' she said, eagerly.

'My father's map room is under guard,' said Florian, 'but Phini magicked us in, and we found it!' He looked lovingly at the blond fairy, and she beamed back at him.

'And?' said Luck, from the bed. He didn't seem inclined to get up.

'The land in the Dark Forest to the east of Queen Rosalind's belongs to a recently deceased Queen,' said Phinella.

'Who'd it pass to?' said Luck.

'Nobody yet,' said Florian. 'It'll go to one of the Queen's three children, but we don't know which. They're our next stop.'

'Seeing as it's impossible to get anything out of *The Powers*,' said Phinella, with a disgusted look.

'We're going now,' said Florian. 'Just wanted to stop by and give you an update first.' The pair seemed energized by their newfound purpose, despite the media storm still swirling around them.

'What if the children refuse to see you?' Storm blurted. 'On account of your recent scandal?'

All eyes turned to Storm, who smiled weakly. Her stomach dropped, and her breaths became shallow, sparrow-like things.

'Hopefully word is yet to reach them,' said Phinella, curtly. 'And if it has, maybe our *scandal* will make them more inclined to meet with us, not less.'

'Yes, of course,' said Storm. 'Sorry.'

'Well, good luck,' said Gamble, impatient for them to be off. 'We'll be here on your return.'

'An' look see if the angels 'ave crossed the boundary already ...' said Luck.

'We have people looking into it, but, well, your magic is ...' Gamble looked at Phinella and waved her hand in a circle, 'superior in terms of speed.'

'Of course,' said Phinella, and then she and Florian disappeared, making no sound, nor rush of air, nor burst of heat. They were simply there one moment and gone the next.

'Isn't magic a marvel!' said Gamble, staring at the space the pair had occupied.

Storm tried to smile, although she wasn't sure her lips obeyed. She had to leave. Had to get out. Phinella and Florian would speak to the heirs, discover the angels were already over the border, then magic the heirs to *The Powers,* find the paperwork, and learn the truth. That Storm was the one who'd granted the angels access to the land. That she was a traitor to her people.

She had to get a message to Gabriel. Had to find a reason to be alone. She still had over a day before the land was officially hers ... before it was no longer legal for challengers to kill her with no consequence.

* * *

Storm waited all morning, watching and hoping for any opportunity to slip away. Finally, Hunter announced he was taking a shower, and moments after the bathroom door closed, Storm headed for the exit, telling the dwarves she needed some air.

If they sent each other troubled looks, Storm didn't see, for her only focus was escape.

As soon as her feet hit the dirt at the bottom of the ladder, she ran, heading deeper into the trees. She yanked open her necklace, sent a flare to summon Gabriel, then mouthed a silent prayer to all the Gods that he would be swift in his rescue.

It wasn't long before Storm's lungs burned, forcing her to slow. She walked and walked, wondering how things had come to this. Her best friend in all the land working against her. Although, that wasn't quite accurate, for Storm knew not what Hunter wanted … who he was working with, or working for. What he was up to …

Gabriel's winged form finally circled the trees above, and Storm frantically waved her arms.

'Gabriel!' she called. His eyes locked with hers as he descended, and a rush of relief filled her.

But then a twig snapped behind her in the trees, and a cruel voice said, 'Going somewhere?'

Storm whirled to face Hunter, who stood with the elf beside him. She couldn't decipher the meaning of Hunter's features, and it sent a shiver of terror down her spine.

'See?' said Hunter. 'I told you.'

'Indeed,' said the elf, stepping forward.

'No further,' said Gabriel, sounding bored. He landed beside Storm and wrapped an arm around her waist, lifting her easily into his hold.

'She's a traitor,' said Hunter, his face a sneer. 'Helping you angel scum.'

Gabriel lifted off into the sky just as Hunter pulled a slingshot from his pocket.

'Gabriel!' Storm breathed.

Hunter let a projectile fly, and Gabriel swerved sharply, narrowly missing the stone, but Hunter reloaded in a moment. He loosed a second stone, and this time, there was nowhere for Gabriel to go, trees blocking him on all sides.

'No!' Storm screamed. She flung her hand out towards the stone, willing it to stop with every fiber of her being. Something shifted inside her, uncoiling, stretching, yawning, time slowing from a torrent to a trickle. And suddenly, she could feel the stone, the disturbance it made as it travelled through the air, the ferocious force behind the weapon.

To her astonishment, she found she could command the stone. But not only that, she could command the air, and the leaves, and the wind, and she felt powerful in the knowledge that there were any number of ways she could prevent it from finding its mark.

She ordered it to stop, throwing some small part of her power back towards it, just to make sure. And it stopped, then fell to the ground.

Gabriel cleared the trees, flying at breakneck speed for the Dark Forest, but Storm barely noticed the rise and fall as he beat his wings, or the wind messing her hair. She stared at her hand, turning it this way and that, her mouth wide open in shock.

'What the fuck did I just do?' she whispered, finally pulling her eyes from her hand to look at Gabriel.

A grin spread across his face. A grin. She'd barely ever seen him smile, and certainly nothing like this.

'What?' she said, utterly baffled.

'I love you,' he said, then pressed his lips to the top of her head.

'Gabriel?' she said, unable to suppress the pang of happiness that filled her.

'You used your power,' he said, the grin back on his face.

'My what?'

'Your magic.'

'I don't have any magic.' At least, she'd never known she did.

'Tell that to the stone you stopped in mid-air.'

'But ...' Storm couldn't think of words, her mind racing while warm gratification filled her chest. He loved her. He'd saved her. 'Thank you,' she breathed.

'Always,' he said, and kissed her hair again.

Gabriel landed on the edge of the angels' mining operation. Everywhere Storm looked was a flurry of activity, angels carrying rocks from the vast holes they'd blasted in the ground, loading them onto the crushers, then sifting the dusty remnants to extract what they'd come for.

'We need to step things up,' said Gabriel, the words out before his feet had even touched the ground.

Michael's face remained neutral. 'Because?' he said, his eyes flicking to Storm.

'Because my flimsy cover is blown to smithereens,' said Storm, 'and soon every royal within a day's radius will be out to kill me.' She said the words flippantly, but the thought made her want to hurl.

Michael raised an eyebrow. 'I'll rally the troops,' he said. 'We're making good time. By tomorrow morning, we should have enough.'

'Good,' said Gabriel, 'because I doubt we've got longer than that.'

Gabriel and Storm rolled up their sleeves and got to work. Gabriel carried load after load from the mine, his shirtless chest rippling in the sun, sweat running in rivulets across the ridges of his muscles. Storm didn't have time to stare, her attention glued to the task of sifting the crushed rock, pulling out the sparkling, transparent crystals the angels needed. She couldn't even find the energy to think about her newfound magical abilities. Or maybe it was that she didn't want to think about them …

The day rolled by, and when the sun's light disappeared, they illuminated glow stones so they could continue through the night. Hours after sunset, Gabriel came to pull Storm from her work, her hands cut and blistered, her skin cracked and dry.

'You need to eat,' said Gabriel, 'and rest.'

A part of Storm wanted to keep going, knowing the faster they mined, the sooner they could leave, but she could barely keep herself upright, so she nodded and took his hand.

Gabriel led her to a shower block, growled at the others to get out, then tugged her in behind him. Storm sent an apologetic look to the half-naked angels who'd been trying to get clean after a full day's work. 'We won't be long,' she said.

Gabriel's eyes darkened. 'Won't we?' His voice was low, so only she could hear.

A shiver travelled down her spine, her nipples tightening under his gaze, and a coy smile spread across her lips, her tiredness all but forgotten.

Gabriel reached in and turned on the water, then he stripped off his dusty, sweat-soaked breeches and let them drop to the floor. She smiled at the sight of his arousal, some base, possessive part of her glad she could invoke such a reaction before they'd even touched.

'Your turn,' he said, her stomach contracting at his commanding tone.

She did as she was told, removing her filthy clothes slowly enough to make him restless.

When she was finally naked, she slinked her hourglass form towards him, one slow step at a time.

They stood toe to toe, and now she was impatient, but he didn't touch her, the feral smile on his lips telling her two could play at her game.

'After you,' he said, holding out his arm towards the shower.

Storm blinked her eyelashes seductively, then stepped past him into the fall of water, an involuntary gasp escaping her lips as the freezing liquid hit her skin.

Gabriel was behind her in an instant, his chest to her back, his arms around her, one hand cupping her breast, while the other explored the dip of her waist. The mix of cold and heat made Storm's head spin and her insides blaze, quiet moans filling the space—her moans, she realized, for Gabriel's lips were sucking at her neck.

She reached up a hand, twining her fingers in his hair, the action arching her back, thrusting her breasts further into his touch. He growled, then slid a hand to her sex, and she cried out as he skated her core, moving her hips to seek friction.

Gabriel huffed a laugh into her neck, then bit her gently, sucking and pulling on her skin, winding her body so tight so thought she might implode. And then he pinched her nipple, and the coil released, sending twists of pleasure through every part of her. It hit again and again, as Gabriel held her to him, grinding against her as he supported her weight.

Knocking sounded from the entrance as her moans subsided. 'Unless you want an audience, it's time to come out now,' said Michael, his tone amused-yet-firm.

Gabriel kept working his fingers, drawing out every last ounce of pleasure, but frustration rumbled through his chest. He tilted her head and captured her lips, pulsing his hips. Storm tipped her head back and exhaled a half-laugh. 'No time,' she whispered. Then she picked up the soap, spun to face him, and lathered up his chest.

They dressed, Gabriel conjuring up a clean smock and pants for Storm that were only a little too big, then finally freed up the showers for the others.

They made for the crackling campfires where the resting angels lounged, but halfway, Storm put a hand on Gabriel's arm, stopping him in his tracks.

He looked down at her, concern written across his features, his face close in the badly lit space. 'What is it?' he asked, taking her hand.

She could still feel him everywhere, and smell him, her brain a lust-filled haze, hard for her to wade through. 'Earlier,' she managed, 'when I stopped the stone from Hunter's slingshot ... what did I do?'

Gabriel leaned down and kissed her, the touch feather-light, but enough to send a shiver down her spine. 'You showed your true self,' he said, then pressed his lips to hers once more, the kiss deeper, more demanding, making her head spin.

She wanted to rub herself against him, to climb into his arms then urge him to kiss every inch of her skin. But she'd put off asking all day. With the threat of an attack, she could do so no longer.

'What do you mean, my *true self*? And how could you know that?'

Gabriel rested his forehead against hers and slid his thumb back and forth along her chin. 'I promise it will become clear very soon ... as soon as we get out of here. For now, just know you're powerful, and magnificent, and terrifying. If an attack comes, you must believe that; don't be scared to show our enemies what you can do.'

He kissed her again, then tugged her behind him. She was still digesting his words as they joined Michael and a group of angels at a fire.

Gabriel pulled her to the ground to sit between his legs, and she leaned back against his chest, his arms settling around her. A part of her wanted to ask him more. What kind of magic did she have? How did he know? What did he mean, it would all become clear? But a greater part of her was satisfied just to be in his arms, to feel safe under his protection, to embrace the contented elation that swelled in her chest.

If the others thought it strange their leader had wrapped himself around her, none of them said anything, nor batted an eyelid. All they seemed to care about was going home.

'Gods, I miss the noodles the guild vendors sell,' said one, biting the end off a carrot.

'I miss my magic,' said another.

'I've had enough of these ridiculous wings,' said a third, spreading them to their enormous span to illustrate his point.

'I miss the peace and quiet in the depths of the mountain.'

'The parties.'

'Friends.'

'You don't have any friends!'

Storm let their banter wash over her, the gentle strumming of a guitar at a nearby fire lulling her until she could keep her eyes open no longer.

Everything went suddenly dark, and the shock jolted Storm awake. But she opened her eyes to find wings shielding her from the world, cocooning her in warmth and comfort, and the sweet, delicious scent of Gabriel.

Storm awoke the following morning to find the air tense. Heavy and electric. Like a storm brewed around them, tight and uncomfortable.

Gabriel was nowhere to be seen. At some point during the night, he'd laid her on a blanket and slipped away, presumably to take another shift in the mines.

Storm didn't delay long before taking her own place, slipping easily back into sifting the crushed rock. Gabriel smiled when he saw her, although there was a tension about his mouth, and he seemed almost jumpy, his eyes flicking to the tree line every few seconds.

He deposited his load, then came to her end of the line and dropped a kiss on her lips. Storm flushed, aware of their considerable audience, but Gabriel didn't seem to care.

'In seven spins of the hand, you'll be safe,' said Gabriel, attempting a reassuring smile.

'Seven hours is a long stretch,' said Storm. The thought of what could happen in that time had her holding her breath. She forced herself to inhale deeply and relax her shoulders. It would be fine. They would mine enough of the gleaming crystals and then run for the House of Portals without a single challenge. That's how things would go down.

'Maybe I can speed things along with my magic,' said Storm, looking down at her hands.

Gabriel smiled and shook his head. 'Grateful as I am that you saved my life yesterday, it would be dangerous to experiment on something so important.'

Storm nodded, knowing he was right. She could just as easily destroy the mine and cost them vital time, but it was so very tempting.

'How much longer?' Gabriel asked Michael.

'A few hours,' he replied. 'Less if we get lucky.'

A few hours. Storm had to survive for only a few short hours. How hard could that be?

Despite the ferocious pace of work, the time passed slowly. They didn't get lucky with the mineral. If anything, they got unlucky, less of the crystals seeming to materialize with each load of rock. Storm checked and rechecked, hoping she'd missed something, but most loads contained barely anything at all. Every time she found a crystal, Storm's heart lurched, but it wasn't enough, and tension rose with every passing minute.

After four arduous hours, Gabriel forced Storm to take a break. He made her drink water and eat a slice of bread folded around some hard, tangy cheese, but she could barely swallow, every part of her strained with worry. They were sitting ducks. The resistance could arrive at any second, or an eligible royal with aspirations of owning a section of the Dark Forest.

'Let's get back,' said Storm, the break doing nothing but causing her to panic.

But Gabriel didn't respond, for he was staring at the tree line. 'Shit,' he said, and Storm whirled to look, her eyes locking on the figures materializing through the trees.

'Gabriel,' Storm said on an exhale, clutching his arm.

'Michael! Keep production going at all costs,' Gabriel called. 'We'll head them off.'

Michael nodded, and the angels increased their pace. Their actions became almost frantic, tiredness chased away by the threat of more time apart from their home and loved ones.

Strangely, Gabriel seemed to relax, like the waiting, the unknown, had been worse than the event itself.

Although they still faced an unknown threat, no clue the size of their opposing force.

And more kept appearing through the trees, presumably magicked in by Phinella, or other fairy godmothers, because who knew how many the resistance had at their disposal?

Florian stepped out of the trees, flanked by three figures Storm didn't recognize, and then Phinella materialized beside them, Luck and Gamble in tow.

'I'd hoped it wasn't true,' said Florian, his perfect princely tone ringing out across the clearing.

'Worried it'll tarnish your reputation when it gets out your true love is working with the angels?' said Storm.

Florian cast a sideways glance at Phinella, who shook her head the smallest fraction.

'We've brought the rightful heirs,' said Florian, motioning to the woman and two men beside him. There was nothing distinguishing about them, aside from their matching expressions of indignity.

'The forest does not belong to them,' said Storm, 'for their mother failed to name an heir, and they could not agree one among themselves.'

'They require time to grieve her loss, that is all,' said Florian. 'They will choose in time.'

Gabriel laughed. 'If you believe that, you are a fool,' he said. 'They are pitiful excuses for royalty, and deserve none of their privilege, least of all this forest. Places like this are not meant for the likes of them.'

'Now look here,' said the taller of the two men.

'How dare you,' said the woman.

The third looked bored, as though he had better places to be, then said, 'You both know I'll end up with the land. Why don't you do us all a favor and agree? Then we can banish this troop of criminals and return to our business.'

'So you can banish us too?' said the woman, her face a scowl.

Her brother shrugged noncommittally.

As they spoke, more figures appeared through the trees, and Storm's heart leapt into her mouth. Their time was up, and they didn't have enough of the mineral. If they didn't extract enough now, they likely never would. And if the angels couldn't complete their mission, would Isaiah let them return to their homeland? Let her return with them?

Storm couldn't take the chance, nor could she live with herself if she didn't do everything in her power, so she felt for her newly discovered magic.

It was easy to find, but slippery. It was as though she skidded across a frozen river, then hit the bank on the other side, coming to an abrupt and jarring halt. She tried again more gingerly, heading for the center, sliding this way and that as she got a feel for it, until the unfurling sensation filled her once more.

She lost control once, twice, then stabilized and reached out to the mine, holding a picture of the crystals she sought in her mind. Her magic rocketed forward, then screeched to a halt as Storm pulled back, terror filling every part of her.

The children were bickering like five-year-olds, making it hard to concentrate. Storm waved a hand to silence them, and they fell to the floor, alive but unable to distract her. She didn't dwell on what she'd done, or where the impulse had come from.

'What the …' said Florian. He stepped forward, but then eyed the figures lying awkwardly on the ground, and his movements became tentative.

Storm returned to her magic, pushing it forward once more, careful this time to keep it steady. Like a child learning to take its first steps, she inched towards the mine, seeking the crystals that hid beneath the rock.

Her magic descended into the cool depths of the mineshaft, and she switched her focus to the crystals, locating them one by one, searching for a load big enough to mean they could escape this hell hole without delay.

'What did you do to them?' said Florian, feeling for a pulse in each of their necks.

'They'll sleep it off,' said Gabriel, although, of course, he couldn't know that.

'In which case,' said Florian, 'I claim this forest as my own. *The Powers* informed us we have only a few hours left to challenge you, and we will not let this destruction stand.' He drew his sword, and a flood of fear filled Storm's chest, distracting her from her task. She didn't know how to fight. She'd only ever been taught to look after the castle and obey the Queen.

'Stop,' Storm said to Florian, just as Phinella magicked herself into the space behind Storm. Phinella made to grab her, but Gabriel got there first. He hauled Phinella into the air and pinned her arms to her sides.

'Put her down!' cried Florian, at the same moment as Phinella said, 'Unhand me!'

'You really want me to do that?' said Gabriel, his lips curling into a cruel smile.

'I can fly, moron,' said Phinella, a hard smile of her own forming on her lips.

Storm acted without thinking, of no doubt that Phinella was about to attack Gabriel with her magic. 'Sleep,' said Storm. She circled her fingers, then pulled them into a ball. Phinella's eyes closed, and Florian howled.

'What have you done to her?' he demanded, his sword arm falling, his true love his only focus.

Storm ignored him and returned quickly to her task, locating the crystals, and then ... *yes, there*. She found a large deposit. She didn't know if it would be enough, but it was something. Although she needed to extract the crystals without hurting those inside the mine ...

'Get her!' shouted a male voice.

Storm broke her concentration long enough to assess their worsening predicament. The trees were now full of figures, some Storm recognized from the Camembert party, and some she'd never seen before.

Screw it. There's no time. Storm yanked with her magic, pulling on the crystals with all her might, until they shot free from the rock and jubilation filled her.

'She'll wake soon enough,' said Gabriel. He sounded confident as he flew Phinella to the other side of the mine and placed her on the ground.

'You're holding her hostage?' Florian spluttered, as though he couldn't quite believe it.

'It is your intention to attack us, is it not?'

Hunter and the elf stepped out of the trees, something deeply menacing about the way they moved.

'You attacked us first,' said Hunter. He held out his hand, which contained a ruby red apple, a strange stick poking out of the top. 'But this ends now.'

Storm couldn't see it clearly from this distance, but whatever it was, she felt the threat deep in her bones, and her feet moved without conscious thought. She ran, escape her only priority, but somewhere in the back of her mind, she heard a pop that sounded like an explosion. It seemed far away, and yet, she felt herself falling, falling, falling. And then everything went black.

* * *

Gabriel watched as Hunter threw the apple. Watched as it bounced on the ground behind Storm's racing feet. Watched as it exploded, splattering her with fragments. Watched as the woman he loved fell to the forest floor.

He saw red, drawing both of the short swords he kept attached to his hips and flying for Hunter. But Hunter clasped the hand of the elf beside him, and they disappeared.

Gabriel roared in fury, whirling back to where Storm lay motionless on the ground. He snatched up the blanket she'd slept on and wrapped it around her, careful not to touch the apple pulp that stained her skin and clothes. Hunter had turned the poisoned apple into an altogether different weapon, but there was no time to dwell on that now.

As Gabriel lifted Storm into his arms, Michael shouted, 'Retreat!' at the top of his lungs.

All around, angels took to the air, weighed down by bags of the precious mineral they'd come for.

Michael would never call a retreat, not given the stakes, which meant ... they had enough. They had enough!

Gabriel tamped down his elation; they still had to make it to the portal, and he didn't know what the modified apple had done to Storm. Maybe she was in mortal danger. Maybe this had all been for nothing ...

Gabriel launched into the air and beat his wings in fast, powerful strokes, casting not a single glance behind him. All that mattered was taking Storm home.

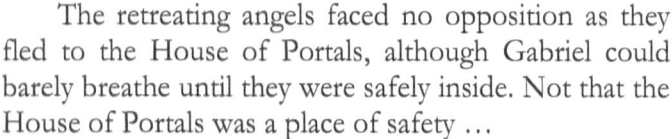

The retreating angels faced no opposition as they fled to the House of Portals, although Gabriel could barely breathe until they were safely inside. Not that the House of Portals was a place of safety ...

Michael had already opened the portal to their world. 'I can't wait to get rid of these wings,' said an angel, gleefully. He stepped through the portal, disappearing from view, and another took his place in front of the swirling black hole.

Gabriel pushed past the line, forcing away the irritation bubbling in his chest, and laid Storm carefully on the ground.

'Just take her through,' said Michael, giving Gabriel an incredulous look. 'Now!'

'I can't,' said Gabriel, a knot forming in his chest. 'I need to tell her ...' What? That he was sorry?

Gabriel placed a light kiss on Storm's lips, and she woke almost at once, her eyes flying open, then going wide. She struggled against him, trying to free her arms, which were trapped by her sides, her whole body still wrapped in the blanket.

'Hang on,' said Gabriel. 'Hold still.' He stepped back, carefully lifted her to her feet, then removed the blanket. 'The apple fragments may still be dangerous.'

Storm picked a piece off her clothes. 'Nope,' she said, then shook her hand violently, sending the apple flying to the ground.

'We're in the House of Portals,' said Gabriel, as the final angel disappeared through the swirling black hole, leaving only Michael, Storm, and Gabriel behind.

'We have enough crystals?' said Storm, her eyes flicking to Michael.

He nodded. 'A large deposit came flying out of the rock just as everything was going to shit. Right between the heads of two angels. Would surely have killed them if they'd been struck ...'

Storm nodded, although her face paled.

'We have to go,' said Michael, eying the portal warily. 'This place is fickle; we shouldn't dally.' His tone was light, presumably for Storm's benefit, but Gabriel didn't miss the words between the lines: *let's get the fuck out of here, you idiot.*

'You go,' said Gabriel. 'We're right behind you.'

Michael looked as though he would protest, then shook his head and stepped through.

'You're having second thoughts about taking me with you?' said Storm, her face so crestfallen his chest clenched.

'No, of course not,' said Gabriel. He stepped into her space and cupped her cheek. 'You remember what I told you about the apple? That true love's kiss is the only cure?'

She nodded slowly, watching him with confusion in her eyes.

'Just …' He paused, then placed a chaste kiss on her lips, wishing he could find some way to explain. 'Just remember that on the other side.'

Gabriel took her hand and pulled her towards the portal, about to step through when the door banged open behind them. 'Stop,' said Hunter, the elf a pace behind.

Gabriel didn't hesitate. Didn't pause to tell them he knew what they were. Instead, he pushed Storm into the portal, then followed her through, breathing a sigh of relief to finally be going home.

Part Two

Chapter Eight

STORM LURCHED INTO THE swirling black, her heart hammering in excited trepidation. If the portal had some effect on her, she couldn't discern it, but when she emerged on the other side, in a dark, dank cavern, everything had changed.

Gabriel came through behind her. He placed a hand on her shoulder, spinning her to face him. 'Storm?' he said, looking deep into her eyes.

Storm looked back, suddenly knowing … so much … too much, and then she let out a scream so loud and so laced with magic that the mountain itself seemed to shake.

'She's back,' said Michael, with a salacious raise of his eyebrow. 'Now the fun begins …'

'Oh, piss off,' said Gabriel.

'I'd rather not,' said Michael.

Storm sent a bolt of magic towards him, sparks hitting the rock by his head. 'I'm rusty,' she said. 'My next one might hit something important.'

Michael retreated with a chuckle. 'I'll report our success to our illustrious leader.'

Storm let out another shriek. 'Why did you come and get me?'

'Because I love you,' said Gabriel.

'Because *Isa* told you to?'

'You were living a delusion,' said Gabriel. 'It wasn't healthy.'

'*Healthy*?' said Storm, with a malicious laugh. 'What part of my life here is *healthy*?'

'I love you,' said Gabriel. 'I don't want to be without you.'

'Yet you care not what I want?'

'You want to live the life of a slave girl, oppressed by a big, bad queen?' said Gabriel, a mocking edge to his tone.

'No different to here,' said Storm, realizing her mistake as soon as the words left her mouth.

'Exactly,' said Gabriel.

'Urggghhhhh,' she shrieked. She balled her hands and sent bolts of magic to the floor so strong the ground cracked.

'Not near the portal,' said Gabriel, fear taking hold of his features.

She did it again, and the ground fractured some more.

'Storm,' he said, pleadingly, then he flew for the tunnel Michael had left through.

'Don't fly away from me!' she screeched. She followed him, sealing the tunnel behind her with a flick of her hand. No one else would be using that portal any time soon.

Storm grabbed Gabriel's shoulders as he entered a larger cavern, this one filled with reunions, those who had been angels now back in their usual forms. Fae, nymphs, and mages hugged their loved ones, overjoyed to be together again.

'Get out!' Storm screamed, the display of what she would never have a sharp slap across her face.

They scattered, Michael hurrying away with a smirk in Gabriel's direction that only stoked the flames of Storm's fury. She sent a bolt of magic at the ceiling, and boulders fell all around them.

'Storm, stop!' shouted Gabriel, stretching out his wings to shield himself from the dust that followed.

'No,' she said. 'I will not.'

She sent a stream of magic into the floor, so much that Gabriel paled. 'Storm, please …' he said. 'We need to talk. Things have changed. The Five Eastern Kingdoms are united. A queen sits on the throne. She's welcoming the magical back to her lands. She seeks the dragons …'

Storm went very still, her mind whirring, processing. 'We can leave?' she said. They'd been stuck here, under this damned mountain, for centuries on end. She longed to escape, leave it and all its baggage behind, to forge a new life … but of course, it was hopeless.

'Isa will never let you go,' she said bitterly.

'We'll find a way,' said Gabriel.

Storm shook her head, and then her brain clicked the pieces into place. 'The Children,' she said, remembering Isa's words through the portal. 'They're acting up. That's the real reason you came for me.' Rage boiled inside her, so she drew back her hand and flung magic at the wall. It felt good, so she did it again, again, again.

'Storm,' said Gabriel. He placed his hands on her shoulders, trying to draw her to him.

'Don't,' she barked, whirling to face him, knocking his hands away.

'I love you,' he said. 'I woke you with true love's kiss …'

'You said it yourself; I was living a delusion.'

'I love you, Storm,' he said. 'No matter what Isa says, or does, or makes me do, she can never change the way I feel about you.'

Storm knew he spoke the truth, but sometimes love simply wasn't enough. 'Try as she may,' said Storm. 'But when she clicks her fingers, you run along regardless.'

'As does every other being under this mountain,' said Gabriel. 'Even you.'

'Not every being,' said Storm, shaking her head. 'Not the Children.' For they answered to nothing and no one, even the mighty Isa. Sure, they could be reasoned with ... but only by Storm.

Michael poked his head inside the cave and eyed them both warily. 'Isa wishes to see you,' he said.

Gabriel ran a hand through his hair. 'We'll be right ...'

'Ah ... not both of you,' said Michael, already making his retreat. 'Only Gabriel.'

Gabriel feared for the structural integrity of the mountain as Storm let fly one stream of magic after another. Her magic was a rare and wonderful thing, but it was also terrifying, destructive, and brutal. Storm had weathered much in her long life, and if she brought the mountain to its knees, it wouldn't be the first colossal structure she'd destroyed in the name of stress relief.

'Run along,' Storm shouted over the deafening booms of her destruction.

In the past, Gabriel had tried to reason with her when she was like this. He'd tried to pull her into an embrace and show her how much he loved her, but every time, he'd nearly lost his wings to her rage. So he

101

made for the tunnel, saying, 'I'll debrief her and be back as soon as I can.' He had no choice but to serve Isa, and Storm knew that; they'd both sworn an oath to their leader.

'Unless she has other plans for you,' said Storm. She screamed in frustration, then hammered her fist into the wall. It cracked, and she screamed again.

'Just … try not to hurt yourself,' he said quietly.

The sound of destruction followed Gabriel as he made his way to Isa's private quarters. He didn't pass a soul as he ascended from the bowls of the mountain, navigating the treacherous tunnels.

Gabriel was the bridge between the long-lives of the depths—those who had only reluctantly acquiesced to Isa's leadership—and the young Fae'ch who lived near the surface. They'd come to the mountain during trying times, when the magical had had nowhere else to go. They'd run from the persecution of the Kings of the Five Kingdoms, their magic weakened after the dragons disappeared. The Kings had all but stamped them out of existence, with contraptions specially designed to lure and trap the magical.

Someone had needed to lead, and Isa had been the best of the choices available. Gabriel had never wanted the role, nor Storm or Michael. Gabriel's plan had been to retreat into the depths of the mountain and live out his life with Storm and his friends, away from Isa's all-seeing gaze.

Isa had had other ideas.

'Come,' said Isa, as Gabriel crossed the threshold into her domain. 'Sit.'

The section of mountain Isa called home was as close to the surface as it could be. She'd had sorcerers alter sections of the rock above, so tiny rays of sunlight made it through, giving the place a gentle glow. It did not suit her, for Isa was anything but gentle.

Gabriel swept his eyes across the cave, each section on a different level, with wide steps connecting the spaces. Not much had changed in his absence, the sleeping, seating, and eating areas much the same as they'd always been.

Isa had no need for a kitchen, for others brought her food, although she rarely remembered to eat. Gabriel shuddered as his eyes slid over the bed, foul memories forcing their way into his mind. If she ever slept, Gabriel had never born witness, but that didn't mean she never used the bed.

'Darling,' said Isa. Her focus, which had wandered elsewhere, snapped back into the room.

There were those in the depths who joked Gabriel was the only creature alive who could command Isa's full attention. It wasn't quite true, but they weren't far off. For Gabriel's part, the attention was unwelcome, although there was little he could do about it.

'Isa,' he said, his voice distant. He didn't bow, for she had lost his respect long ago.

'Oh. Come now. My love. Don't be like that.' Her voice followed a halting path, meaning she still wasn't totally with him, her mind partly elsewhere, watching some other happening under the mountain. 'It has been many spans. Since we last saw. One another.'

Not nearly long enough.

'Perhaps we should become reacquainted …' she said, her voice becoming fluid.

Shit. The threat was thinly veiled. It had been many turns of the sun since she'd last forced him, but the mere mention was enough to make him play her game. He inclined his head. 'Michael debriefed you?'

'Come sit by me,' she said. She flicked her auburn hair over her shoulder as she sank onto the leather cushions, and her lips curled into a feline smile.

Gabriel's thoughts turned to Storm, wondering what she was doing in his absence. The mountain no longer shook, which was probably a good sign, but then again, maybe it meant she was plotting something worse …

He reluctantly moved to Isa's side, sitting as far from her as he could without making a point.

'Now, my love,' she said, the words making his skin crawl, 'tell me all.'

My love. Isa's fae line was well known for their magical attachments, believing they were merely conduits for the magic, that it was their sacred duty to mate with whomever the magic propelled them towards. Isa's magic had chosen Gabriel—or so she said—and he could do little to protest, her power supreme, at least while they remained under the mountain.

Had Gabriel or Storm wanted to lead, Isa never would have stood a chance, but all they'd wanted was to disappear into the depths together. Isa had waited until after they'd sworn oaths to obey her to tell them of her attachment to Gabriel. An attachment that would last until her soul fled the mortal world.

Gabriel had rejected her in every way he knew how, but she was their leader. He'd sworn an oath. And Isa hadn't been afraid to use that oath against him.

He'd once felt sorry for her, and his pity had blinded him to her black, malicious soul. Had he not been so stupid as to put himself at her mercy, he would stab a dagger in her heart and not think twice.

'Come, my love,' she said, her voice a purr. 'Don't keep me waiting.'

It had been a long time since Isa had been like this. Did she plan to compel him into her bed? Or make him perform other unsavory acts?

'Michael must have told you,' said Gabriel, his voice crisp and to the point. 'We mined the crystals and retrieved Storm, just as you requested. Storm isn't happy about it.'

'So I gather,' said Isa, with an imperious shrug. 'She has always been … difficult.'

'The situation is difficult for us all,' said Gabriel, his voice sharper than was wise.

Isa's eyes turned hard. She leaned forward and ran a finger down his bicep. 'Hardest for me,' she said, 'for I am bound by magic to love you. At least she has a choice.'

Did Storm have a choice? Gabriel wasn't sure that was how love worked. Long ago, when Isa had chosen Gabriel, she'd known there was no other way to have him. How much had been magic, and how much had been spite? If it was spite, as he suspected, Isa had chosen this hell in a way he and Storm had not. Maybe she'd convinced herself Gabriel would leave Storm after she'd backed them into a corner, or that Storm would leave him …

'If you would just give in to the magic,' she said, then lifted his hand to her lips and kissed his palm. Gabriel fought the urge to slap her, or fly for the door and refuse to return. But he'd tired it before. Isa would use magic to still his wings, and then pull him back like a fish on a line.

Isa went up on her knees and moved his hand to her hip. Gabriel's breaths became short, panicked puffs. She wouldn't … hadn't for decades …

'If you would just embrace that we are meant to be together,' she said, leaning down, her lips approaching Gabriel's.

'I do not want this,' Gabriel breathed, his stomach churning. He turned his head away, but Isa slid a finger under his chin and pulled him back, using magic when he refused to comply.

'Now is the time for us to have a child,' said Isa. 'I feel it. We high fae must bolster our ranks.'

Gabriel's stomach churned. He was no *high fae*; there was no such thing, at least not before Isa's mother had created the echelon. 'Like you felt it before?' he mocked, unwelcome memories flashing before his eyes.

'The magic was testing us, and we did not pass,' she said. '*You* did not pass. You must learn to obey, to heed the wishes of the one you are destined to love.'

'I am not destined to love you,' Gabriel ground out, just as the circular metal door burst open.

Storm flew for Isa, hurtling through the air without the need for wings. She stopped a hair's breadth from Isa's face, then screamed at the top of her lungs, 'He loves me!'

'No,' said Isa. 'You are merely a test.'

This time, when Storm screamed, there were no words. She lifted her hands and punched towards Isa, but they ricocheted back, the magic of Storm's oath preventing her from meeting her mark. Storm punched over and over, and Isa simply sat there, watching as though bored.

'Storm,' said Gabriel, soothingly, trying to snap her out of her frenzy. It did nothing to quell her, so he stood and slipped an arm around her waist, pushing her back a pace, putting himself between Storm and Isa.

Storm shifted her focus to Gabriel, raining punch after punch on his torso. She used a fraction of her true strength, so he didn't try to stop her, but embraced the pain, letting it chase away the lingering feel of Isa on his skin.

He pushed her back another pace, two, using his body to force her away from their leader, to get himself away, too. 'Storm …' he said again. Storm shoved back against him, then rested her palms on his chest, meeting his gaze with scorching eyes.

Gabriel swayed towards her, his eyes glued to her face. She was all he wanted; not Isa, or power, or any of the other things magic had bestowed upon him. The months Storm had been away, living her delusion, had been the hardest of his life. And then, when he'd joined her in the other world, unable to touch her, or kiss her …

Their lips crashed together, and Gabriel buried his hands in her hair. He knew it was unwise, with Isa watching their every move, but he didn't care. He needed to feel her against him, to take everything she gave, for her anger could return at any moment, and then only the Gods knew what she would do … how long she would hold him at arm's length. He had to take every chance to remind her how good they were together.

He moved them towards the door, praying Isa would let them go, whether out of embarrassment or pity he didn't care, so long as they could escape. So long as he could keep Storm pressed against him, taste her skin, show her how much he loved her. How he loved *only* her.

'Enough,' said Isa, her voice a shard of ice, shattering Gabriel's naïve hopes.

Gabriel sucked one last time on Storm's bottom lip, then pulled back. 'I love you,' he whispered, then wrapped an arm around her.

Storm grabbed a handful of his shirt and held on tight, and relief hit Gabriel square in the chest. They were here, together, the same forbidden team they'd always been.

'If you ever do that again,' said Isa, 'I will banish you from the mountain.'

'You need Storm's help,' said Gabriel, as Storm said, 'Given the Five Kingdoms are under new stewardship, I have half a mind to leave of my own accord.'

Gabriel pinched Storm's back, and she exhaled a laugh. The one thing Isa could not do was order them to stay, but she could command them to complete tasks to frustrate their efforts to leave. Of course, it wasn't possible for Isa to command everyone at the same time, so if they left en masse, there was only so much she could do, but in Gabriel's case, Isa would make it a priority to keep him.

'The Children of the Lake have grown restless,' said Isa, her features strained. 'You must broker stability.'

'I doubt that's possible,' said Storm.

'You had better hope it is,' said Isa, although less forcefully than before. Now Storm had somewhere else to go, Isa would have to walk a more careful line.

'Then I need Gabriel's help with the crystals,' said Storm.

It was a lie, but if Isa knew, she chose not to argue. Instead, she waved her hand, dismissing them. She waited until they were crossing the threshold before adding, 'Oh, Gabriel, my love, your son recently joined us under the mountain.'

Isa disappeared, a malicious smirk painted across her face, and Storm shoved Gabriel away. 'Your son?' she said, her voice quiet and menacing.

'I ...' Gabriel faltered, seeming unsure.

'You have a son?' Storm pressed, although the look on his face took the wind out of her sails. He was crestfallen, desolate even.

Gabriel turned and headed for the door without another word, and guilt hollowed out Storm's insides. Hadn't he known? Was Isa really so cruel?

Storm hurried after Gabriel and slipped her hand into his. He clutched it, then used it to pull her into an embrace, burying his nose in her neck.

'I'm sorry,' said Storm. Sometimes she forgot the hell with Isa was just as bad for him … worse, in fact. When it had become too much to bear, Storm had escaped to another world for a while, and even now, she could leave the mountain. But Gabriel couldn't, for Isa would never let him cross the mountain's threshold. Not to mention, he had to deal with her supposed love, running whenever she clicked her fingers.

'I didn't know,' said Gabriel. 'I … she …' He took a long breath. 'She always wanted a baby.' He paused, his arms tightening around her, squeezing her everywhere, his wings wrapping them in a cocoon of black.

Storm stroked his back, then grabbed handfuls of his shirt, her heart beating a frantic rhythm in her chest.

'Of course, it never happened,' said Gabriel. 'Isa blamed me and said my seed must be weak. So she forced me to …' He took a shuddering breath. 'She forced me to have sex with a human woman to test her theory.'

Storm clutched him tighter. He rarely shared the details of what Isa made him do; it was less painful for them both that way. Storm knew it was bad, but this …

'The woman was willing,' he said, his tone firm. 'She had come to the mountain because she wanted a magical father for her child. Isa was titillated by the idea, and it spoke to her vanity, playing God … determining bloodlines.'

'I'm so sorry,' said Storm, not knowing what else to say. If only they'd stopped Isa in the beginning, had refused to let her lead …

'I never knew if the woman got with child,' said Gabriel. 'Isa implied once that she did, but I didn't know for sure, and I wouldn't give her the satisfaction of asking.'

'But now he's here,' said Storm. 'Because Isa wants another way to control you?'

'She already has control,' said Gabriel. 'She doesn't need him for that.'

'Then, why?'

Gabriel pulled back. 'I don't know.'

'Will you meet with him?'

Gabriel stiffened, staying quiet for several long moments. 'It wasn't the child's fault. It would be cruel to punish him for the actions of others, and I'm curious to meet him.'

Storm nodded. He was right, of course, but everything about the situation made her uneasy. Not to mention, it made her wonder what else Isa had hidden up her sleeve.

Chapter Nine

GABRIEL AND STORM RETURNED to the depths of the mountain, a place where Isa rarely ventured, for she knew she wasn't welcome. The long-lives had to bow to her authority like everyone else, but they did so under duress, and that wasn't good for Isa's ego. And now, if Isa pushed them too hard, they would leave, for her jurisdiction spread to the mountain's edge and not an inch beyond.

'Glad to see you two have made up,' said Michael. He eyed their joined hands as they entered the communal space they shared with a few other long-lives.

Many long-lives survived in the depths, keeping to themselves, most of them forgotten by those living out their lives above. They dwelled in groups, supporting one another, helping to alleviate the boredom, keeping alive the traditions their people had always cherished.

And then there were those who made even the long-lives look young. Ancient creatures who had occupied the mountain long before the Fae'ch had sought refuge there. Mostly they dwelled beneath, content to live apart, so long as the Fae'ch did the same. Those creatures knew the balance of power tipped in their favor, for it was only their benevolence that had saved the Fae'ch from the persecution of the old Kings.

So there were those who did not answer to Isa. In fact, Isa answered to them. She had no choice but to pander to their wishes or face eviction from the mountain. But the Children of the Lake were different to the others, for they were not content to live apart, they were not straightforward in expressing their wishes, and they did not like Isa one bit.

Michael sifted through the crystals they'd brought through the portal, and Storm cringed at the thought of the damage they'd done to retrieve them. There would be a price to pay if they ever wanted to use the House of Portals again.

'Why, though?' said Michael, watching her with intense eyes.

'What?' said Storm. 'Why what?'

'Why did you choose that gods-forsaken world to run to?'

Storm shook her head and rolled her eyes. 'I didn't.'

'Then …'

'I asked the House of Portals to take me somewhere I could forget,' she said. Although it hadn't given her the escape she'd truly sought. 'How did you find me?'

'We asked nicely,' said Michael.

'And made an eye-watering donation of imp-cap mushrooms to the House,' said Gabriel.

Storm huffed in frustration; apparently anyone could be bought.

'Tell me what you need,' said Michael, 'assuming you plan to help with the Children?'

'Of course I plan to help. What choice do I have?'

'You could leave,' said Michael. 'The Five Kingdoms are open to our kind once more.'

Storm scoffed. She couldn't leave, not while the Children were restless. She could feel it in the air, their angst and worry, so much more acute than ever before. Along with something else ... bigger, and altogether more terrifying. She marveled the others couldn't feel it too, viscous as it was.

'I swore an oath,' said Storm, 'although if magic is truly welcome in the outside world, my time here is coming to an end.' But there was much the human Queen would have to do before Storm would ever step outside the mountain. Whether Queen Fyia had the knowledge, the fortitude, the luck ... only time would tell.

Gabriel pressed his lips to the back of Storm's hand, and her stomach flipped. Would he ever leave? 'I need to speak with the Children,' said Storm, pushing the thought aside, 'and to know what has happened in my absence.' She turned expectantly to Michael.

Michael raised his eyebrows. 'A lot has happened in your absence.'

'Such as?'

'The Children became hungrier and more frustrated. Isa ran out of all the things they like, and thought the only option was to feed them dragon scales.'

'The only option according to whom?' said Storm.

'Axus,' said Michael.

Axus was Isa's right hand under the mountain. He was a young fae compared to them, but old enough to command respect from the short-lives up top. He had always doted on Isa, and was rumored to be her lover as well as her workhorse, although he'd had at least two children with another fae.

'Axus is an idiot,' said Storm. 'Dragon scales are a drug to the Children. The more they have, the more they need. Anything that potent must be tempered with crystals.'

'Yes, but they ran out of crystals,' said Michael.

'Then why not find some other magical object to feed them? Something with only a hint of magic?'

Michael shrugged. 'Axus was in charge, and I wasn't here.'

'Be that as it may,' said Storm, 'Axus has made them stronger. They feed on magic, but any more than a sliver bloats them … makes them drunk. We must wean them off the scales.'

'Onto what?' said Michael.

'Has anyone asked the other long-lives if they have anything we could use?' said Storm.

Each pocket of Fae'ch who lived in the depths produced something of note. From artwork and pottery, to knives and shields, to the finest cloth spun from silk of the vicious rockhoppers of the deep.

'Sounds like Axus tried, at least a little,' said Michael, 'but he doesn't like to admit when he needs help, and with the new Queen, everyone is restless; it's spooking even the most levelheaded of Fae'ch.'

Storm nodded, but it wasn't the new Queen causing the disturbance in the air. Not unless she was something altogether different from what she seemed …

Storm closed the door to the group of caves she and Gabriel had shared since they'd first moved into the mountain, and some small sense of relief washed over her as they shut out the world.

She waved her hand, and the prisms they'd painstakingly embedded in the ceiling sprang to life, casting the room in a kaleidoscope of color that bounced off the walls.

Gabriel grinned, his shoulders finally relaxing as he moved towards her, wrapping her in his arms. He inhaled deeply, and she hummed at the feel of his hands gliding up and down her back.

'I'm sorry,' he murmured, his lips against her hair.

'Me too,' she said. 'For running away, and for all the shit Isa's done to us both.'

'Why did you go?' he said, squeezing her tighter, as though worried she might disappear.

Storm closed her eyes. 'It … got too much. I couldn't take it any longer and had to … to breathe. When we let Isa lead, we never imagined this is what our lives would become. We never wanted this, and the House of Portals was the only place I could think to go where I'd be able to come back some day. The only place I wouldn't truly be leaving you.'

'But that's exactly what you did,' said Gabriel. He pulled back, letting Storm see the hurt and anger in his eyes.

'You knew where I'd gone,' she said, tamping down the trickle of annoyance leaching into her blood, 'and it was never meant to be forever. But I was so angry. I would have imploded. I needed relief.'

'Why that world? And a situation so similar to …'

'The House has a cruel sense of humor. I didn't specify where I wanted to go, or the life I wanted to lead. I wasn't running towards. I was running away.' Shame heated her cheeks, for it made her a coward. 'But I'm guessing the House is pretty pissed now, given the destruction we caused.'

'Blame Michael,' said Gabriel. 'He found the mineral. All I cared about was finding you.'

'I wonder what's happening there now …'

Gabriel's forehead pinched. 'I couldn't give a damn.'

A memory popped into her head. 'Wait, Hunter and the elf were in the House of Portals … they tried to stop us leaving.'

'Meaning they either followed us, knew about the House all along, or they were as much imposters in that world as we were.'

'You think the latter?' said Storm, judging by his tone.

'I do,' said Gabriel.

'But why?' said Storm, her mind racing. 'My memories are hazy, but I'm pretty sure Hunter was around all the time I was there. You think he was spying on me?'

Gabriel shrugged. 'Or maybe you were a cover. He went after a poisoned apple …'

'And changed it into a much more destructive weapon,' said Storm, cutting him off. 'You think they're arms dealers?'

'Or maybe they work for the House,' said Gabriel. 'But as I said, I couldn't give a damn. They are behind us, and you sealed up the tunnel leading to the portal.'

He moved into her space, crowding her, and Storm smiled with anticipation. She cocked an eyebrow as he came even closer, and when his lips connected with hers, her whole body molded into him, sighing with contentment, for she was home.

Storm pushed him back, then pulled her tunic over her head. She still wore the too-big clothes Gabriel had given her in Fairy Land, and was glad to be rid of them, peeling everything from her skin until she stood naked before him.

'I'm going to take a bath,' she said. 'Would you like to join me?'

Gabriel snatched Storm up into his arms and kissed her deeply. She wrapped her legs around him, and his hands settled on her ample behind, squeezing and kneading.

He carried her away from the large, circular cave where they lived and slept into a side cave. A waterfall tumbled through holes in the wall and ceiling, hitting a deep plunge pool in the floor. Steam spiraled up in wisps, for the waterfall was cold, but the pool was warm, fed by a hot spring below. Colorful stalagmites pushed up from the floor, and stalactites clung to the ceiling.

Storm waved her hand, and the prisms they'd placed around the pool's perimeter glowed a gentle orange, cozy and inviting.

Gabriel dropped Storm back to her feet, and she sashayed towards the pool, moaning when her feet dipped below the surface.

Gabriel pulled at his clothes, naked in record time, but he didn't rush to join her. Instead, he watched, entranced, as she went deeper into the water, walking backwards so her eyes never left his.

She waded until she was up to her neck, then lay back, floating, her body sucking up the restorative warmth.

Storm watched Gabriel as he watched her. He didn't blink, and her heart lurched in her chest.

She closed her eyes, the noises of the cave distorted, the plunging, churning water blocking out all other sounds.

And then a different disturbance rippled through the liquid. A smile tugged at her lips as a shadow fell over her closed eyelids, a shiver racing across her skin as Gabriel's cold finger traced a line across her chest.

Storm let her arms float out to either side, so Gabriel had to move in order to avoid them. She tracked him through the ripples, her body both languid and tense as she anticipated his next touch.

His hands gently pushed apart her feet, and Storm's skin tingled as heat rushed to her core. He ran a finger from her ankle to her knee, and she had to fight to stay relaxed, to keep floating.

A burst of cool water hit her inner thigh—droplets from the waterfall—and Storm bit her lip, willing him higher. He obeyed her silent request, tricking cold along her skin, all the way to the apex of her thighs. She almost convulsed when it hit her there, once, twice, but then he stopped and wrapped her legs around his shoulders.

He floated her until her back rested on the pool's sloped side, but before Storm could become accustomed to the uncomfortable surface, Gabriel lowered his lips to her core, chasing all thoughts of anything but the feel of him from her mind. She bucked against him, her breath hitching as he nipped and sucked, her feet clawing at his back.

Gabriel turned her over, so her breasts pressed against the cold stone. He entered her with one long movement, and Storm moaned, the sound echoing around them. He stilled, his powerful thighs warming the backs of her legs, his chest covering her back. He ran his fingers down her neck, then kissed her there, and Storm pushed back against him, urging him to move.

He traced his fingers down the sides of her breasts, her torso, then grasped her hips and pumped into her with small, exquisite movements.

'Gabriel,' she breathed, gripping the uneven floor to hold herself in place. 'Yes … Gabriel …'

Gabriel grunted in reply, his movements less rhythmic, less controlled, more desperate. 'Storm,' he said. '*Warrior* ...' He thrust forward once more, twice, and then she fell apart, and he came with her.

Gabriel rested his body between Storm's legs and lay his head on her stomach. She reclined on the goose down pillows and ran her hands through his hair. If only their lives were this simple all the time. If only there was no third wheel in their bed ... a wheel with spikes.

'What was with the biting?' said Gabriel, nipping her belly. 'I can't believe you made me bite disgusting Queen Rosalind.'

Storm wanted to laugh, but the memory of Gabriel's lips and hands and teeth on yet another woman made her nauseous. 'That was you, not me.'

'What?' he said, his head snapping up.

'I walked in when you were biting Isa once. I suppose the memory must have stuck in your mind.'

'So when I did those things ...?' said Gabriel.

'That was all you,' said Storm, 'coupled with whatever effect Fairy Land and my delusion had on you. I don't know if Queen Rosalind knew the truth, or if she and the others were even truly real, but your interactions with her were entirely your own. I asked the House of Portals to put me in a delusion, but I didn't ask for power over others. Even if I had, I don't think that's something the House would or could have granted. I don't think they have that power.'

'Oh, Gods,' said Gabriel. 'I'm sorry. I thought you ...'

'I would never make you put your hands on another woman,' said Storm, hotly. 'It is not pleasant for me.'

Gabriel crawled across Storm's body to sit beside her, then took her hand in his. 'I'm sorry,' he said. 'I know that's not enough, but ...'

Storm closed her eyes. Gabriel hadn't meant to hurt her. He loved her, but he was too used to doing the bidding of others; Isa had conditioned him well. Gabriel had no choice with their leader, but he had to break the habit with others.

'I fell in love with you because you thought for yourself, and usually chose the right path,' said Storm. 'The honest, moral path. Don't let Isa erase who you are.'

Gabriel closed his eyes and tipped his head back against the padded headboard. Storm didn't need pretty words and promises—they were past that ... had been for centuries—she needed him to be the Gabriel she loved. He squeezed her hand, and she rested her head on his shoulder, and they sat there in silence for a while.

'I'm leaving,' said Storm. She lifted her head and got to her feet.

'To see the Children?' said Gabriel. A look of confusion spread across his face, presumably due to her overly aggressive tone.

'Yes, but also the mountain.' She grabbed fresh clothes from a chest next to the wall.

'Now?' said Gabriel, jumping up and searching for clothes of his own.

'After I've dealt with the Children,' she said. 'We can go back home ... to our real home by the sea. The new Queen of the Five Kingdoms says she will welcome our kind. I will pave the way for our people and leave this damned place behind.' She stopped dressing and looked deep into his eyes. 'I want you to come with me. For us to find a way.'

Gabriel held her gaze for a beat, two, the weight of her words settling around them. For a terrifying moment, she thought he would refuse, that he would choose Isa, but then he took her hand and pulled her into his arms. 'We can go home,' he agreed, like the idea had only just occurred to him. 'We can leave all this behind.'

'It won't be easy,' said Storm. 'Isa will try to stop you. She has your *son* …' Storm choked on the word. 'And something out there is restless. Something big. I can feel it, and I'm guessing the Children can too.'

No one had a word for the kind of magic Storm possessed. They knew only that she was wildly powerful, and the only being alive who could reason with the Children of the Lake. But whatever she was, she could feel a disturbance in the air like others could feel the coming of a squall, when the sky darkened and the air became charged and heavy. And right now, the tentacles of something magical were stretching across their world, and whatever it was, it was big, and it was nasty, and it was hungry.

* * *

The Children knew Storm was back under the mountain. They would have felt the very moment she stepped through the portal, but she couldn't seem too eager, and she wanted to know exactly what Axus had done in her absence. So when Storm left Gabriel, she sought Isa's right hand.

He was in the great hall—a place Storm hadn't visited for many decades. She avoided the upper levels as a general rule, much preferring the company of the long-lives below, for they remembered the time before … when their lives had had purpose, far from the pitiful, banal husks they were today.

'He's gone,' Axus said to his son, Regio, his tone urgent.

'What do you mean, he's gone?' said Regio, who was the kind of fae artists dreamt of capturing: tall, broad, with blue eyes, razor cheekbones, and dark hair. It was a pity his personality didn't match his image, or so the gossip said.

'Isa sent him away with the Water Rider,' said Axus, his voice low.

'With Alba?' said Regio, practically spitting the name. 'She's not even a long-life …'

'Our leader may do as she pleases,' said Axus, pulling his tall, reedy frame up to its full height. 'It is not for you to question.'

'Ooh, no,' said Storm, sardonically. 'One mustn't do that …'

Axus and Regio whirled towards Storm, and Axus' face fell, his brown eyes gaining a tinge of green. 'Storm,' he said. 'I heard you were back.'

'And I heard you've been amping the Children up on dragon scales,' she said.

'Sussssh,' said Axus, casting his eyes nervously around.

'I suppose that makes sense,' said Storm. 'I'd be embarrassed too, if it were me.'

Axus scowled, but Regio smiled.

'It's not enough,' said Axus. 'They need more and more, and we do not have enough.'

'I'll be the judge of what they require,' said Storm, 'and it is not more scales, of that we can be sure.'

'Then … what?' said Regio, cocking his head to one side. 'We have nothing else to offer them.'

'Not yet, we don't,' said Storm, 'but we will. Gather the water riders—every last one you can find—and meet me by the lake in two turns.'

Axus visibly bristled at the order, but nodded his head. 'As you wish,' he said.

Storm turned just as a man with a stripe of golden scales across his face appeared from the tunnel that led to the lake. 'That's the Queen's brother, is it not?' said Storm, looking to Axus for an answer. Michael had told her about him, and the mystery of why Isa had allowed him to live inside the mountain.

'His name's Veau,' said Regio. 'Barely any magic …'

Storm stopped listening. She made a beeline for the man, leaving the others behind.

'Axus!' said Veau. His face set hard, but Storm intercepted him before he could reach Isa's lap dog.

'You're the Queen's brother?' said Storm. He looked wary as his eyes flicked to take her in. 'I'm Storm.'

'Veau,' he said with a reserved nod.

'I have questions I should like to ask you,' she said, 'about your sister, and the Five Kingdoms.'

Veau's expression turned guarded. 'Why?'

'You'll find out,' said Storm. 'Don't fret, it's nothing bad. I have somewhere to be, but come to the lake in two turns. We will speak then.'

Storm didn't wait for a response. He would come, the temptation too great, and he could have little else of interest to occupy his time.

Chapter Ten

STORM MADE HER WAY around the side of the lake, her eyes always half on the water, ever respectful of the ancient creatures of the deep. For although the Children of the Lake were some of the most feared, plenty of horrors lurked below.

Axus had told her where he usually fed the Children, in a small side cave away from the main lake. It was a good spot for them, although he'd allowed the Children to call all the shots, and that had been the beginning of the loss of Storm's hard-won equilibrium. There was no controlling the Children, but they craved balance in all things, much the same as anyone.

Storm slipped into the side cave, happy to leave the open water behind, and lit a torch to illuminate the small space. At the edge of the cave sat a small pool of water—an offshoot of the main lake—where the Children hid.

Storm approached the water slowly, carefully, but stopped a pace away. She fished a pebble out of her pocket and tossed it into the water. The stone landed with a gentle plop, and then silence fell once more.

'I know you're there,' said Storm, with half a laugh. 'Are you angry with me?'

She tossed another pebble, this one tinged red in places, the flecks of ruby betraying its precious core. The surface rippled, and then the stone hurtled back out of the water. It would have hit her square in the jaw if she hadn't ducked just in time.

Storm laughed. 'You are angry! You shouldn't be, because I have a story to tell, *and* I brought presents from a foreign land.'

Lights played under the surface, and Storm smiled, elation bubbling in her chest the same way it always did when she first saw them.

'My old friends,' she said. She threw a crystal specked with indigo, the most prized of all the gems. Almost as good as dragon scales …

The surface shivered and rippled, and Storm worried they would reject this one as well. If they did, she would have to rethink her plan, and it would mean the situation was far worse than she'd let herself imagine.

But although the water shook as though angry, the crystal remained under. Storm exhaled. 'And that wasn't even the best of it,' she said, somehow keeping her tone light. 'I always look after you, for you are my only true friends.'

The lights circled under the water, glowing silver and pink, and finally a coppery purple that gave Storm hope. Her lips widened into an involuntary smile as the lights began to rise, circling all the while. They circled first clockwise, then switched, spinning back the other way, flicking back and forth as they made their slow ascent.

They finally broke the surface, still rising, moving without check until they were on a level with Storm's eyes. Each was no bigger than Storm's balled fist, and they glowed a multitude of colors as they hovered by her face.

One turned an angry red as they slowed their circle, and Storm's eyes locked onto it. It was the oldest of the five Children, slightly smaller than the rest, and their leader. The Child was angry, Storm's gift fast fading to a memory.

'Did you miss me as I missed you?' she said to the red light. 'I thought of you often.'

'Lies,' said a voice that seemed to hang in the air. Storm knew not if they spoke the words aloud, for she'd never brought another to the Children.

'No,' said Storm. 'I would never be so stupid as to lie to you.' Dragon scales made them volatile, and it had been a while since their last fix. Withdrawal meant they were angry, jittery, irrational.

'You ran from your lovers' quarrel with never a second thought for us,' said the voice.

'Let us not fight,' said Storm. 'Tell me how things have been here. Tell me your troubles.'

'Ha! You care not for our troubles. You care only for yourself … and that we might make trouble for all.'

'I care not if you make trouble for Isa,' said Storm, with a wicked smile. 'I would welcome that. Although you're right, I would not like trouble for myself, or for those who live in the deep. But I am sure I can make you happy. Tell me, what will it take, my friends? What troubles you?'

'Many things,' said the Children. Several voices spoken as one.

'There are too many beasts in the water,' said one.

'It is hot and crowded,' said another.

'Our food is uninteresting,' said a third.

'We want more dragon scales,' said a fourth.

Then, after a weighty pause. 'Something is coming,' said the oldest, the voice more gravely than the rest. 'And when it comes, we will leave the water.'

Storm shied back, the movement involuntary. 'You'll …'

'You heard me. We will not survive in the water. We have no choice but to leave.'

'But …'

'Something is coming,' the voice said again.

'What?' breathed Storm. 'What is coming?'

'Death,' said another of the Children.

'Fire and fury,' said another.

'The end of all as we know it,' said another.

'How do you know this?' said Storm. She felt the disturbance too, but this seemed specific, like they knew details. 'Tell me all you know.'

'We may … in time,' said the oldest. 'But first, you will feed us.'

'I have a spectacle planned especially for you,' said Storm, her heart thundering in her chest. 'I will provide you with a delicacy you have not tasted in a hundred years.'

Silence descended, the weight of it pressing in on Storm, crushing her lungs.

'We will watch your spectacle,' the oldest said eventually, 'but we make no promises. Not to you.'

Storm left the cave with as much dignity as she could muster, sucking in a deep lungful of air as soon as she was out of sight. She leaned against the rock, tipping her head back and washing her face with her hands. It was bad; they no longer trusted her, and she had only a short time to win them back.

They were ancient, time of little consequence, but there was an urgency she'd never felt from them before. Whatever was brewing, it was coming soon. She brushed the thought away; there was nothing she could do about that now, but it was all the more reason to get the hell out of the mountain.

A crowd had gathered at the shallow end of the lake, where water riders rode the lake serpents. The scarier creatures of the deep avoided the area, crowded as it was, meaning it was a good place for inexperienced riders to train.

Storm spotted Axus, Regio, and Veau in the crowd, and she nodded to them, although when she addressed the group, her tone was cold and businesslike. 'I am glad you could come at such short notice,' Storm started, 'for it is no exaggeration to say we face an existential threat.'

Storm watched their reactions closely. Some gasped, some laughed, one or two even rolled their eyes. She'd put those cocky idiots up first …

'You may not believe me,' said Storm, 'but if we fail, you will find out firsthand. And you should know, I want to be here not at all. I am only here because I believe wholeheartedly in the danger.'

No one rolled their eyes this time. It was possible some of the younger ones didn't yet know who she was. But she trusted soon they would, for Storm's relationship with Gabriel, and more to the point, that she was stuck between Isa and Gabriel, was scandalous enough for rumors to spread like lightning.

'I called for water riders because I have a mission for you,' Storm continued. 'One that will appease the Children and bring us back into balance with those ancient and powerful beings.'

Regio cast a glance at his father, and Axus meet his gaze. They seemed hesitant, and the mere hint of dissent made Storm's blood boil. 'Axus,' said Storm, 'I see you sniggering in the back. By all means, take over. If I cannot count on your help, I shall leave you in charge and retire back to the depths, where I am much more at home.'

Storm turned and headed for the tunnels, but Axus' spluttering voice stopped her. 'Apologies if I appeared … disrespectful,' said Axus. 'I certainly meant no offense. We are lucky to have your assistance in this delicate matter.'

Storm spun back to face them, noting the confused expressions. They respected Axus—even though he was a moron—and Storm could use that.

'And?' said Storm.

'And I will punish any who stands in your way, or who laughs, undermines you, or does anything other than give you their full, unwavering attention.'

Storm smiled. That was better than she'd expected. 'Good,' said Storm, striding back to the group. 'Now we have that unpleasantness out of the way, I will share our mission.'

Storm folded her arms as she appraised them, aware her short stature and curves made her look weak and homely. A couple of female fairies returned her gaze, along with one female fae and a female pixie, but aside from that, the group was all male. Not how it had been in times gone by … water riding had been dominated by women, their movements fluid and intuitive.

The silence reached absurdity, and the crowd looked to one other, like they might have missed something. 'Our mission,' said Storm, 'is to rouse a slumbering beast from the deep, with scales so rare they're prized almost as highly as the scales of a dragon.'

One or two looked excited, some blank, but most wore expressions of terror. Storm scowled. 'Where are the real water riders?' she said, rounding on Axus. 'The ones with the magic of the water? The ones who would bite my hand off for an offer such as this?'

Storm wondered if this was Axus' idea of a practical joke. Had he hidden the water riders? But the crowd looked blankly around, and Storm realized it was far worse than that.

'No …' said Storm. 'There aren't any?'

Axus shrugged. 'What good are water riders?'

'What good are water riders?' she repeated, her disbelieving tone snappy, borderline petulant. 'They'd come in useful right about now, don't you think?'

Axus made a few spluttering sounds, then said, 'This isn't a run-of-the-mill occurrence …'

'What other skills have died out because you—or Isa—didn't deem them necessary?' said Storm. 'I knew you placed unwarranted valued on fae magic—weak as that has become—but I never dreamed …'

'There was one,' said Regio. 'At least, I think that's what she was.'

A few of the others began nodding their heads, then a few more, as though working out the meaning of Regio's words.

'Alba,' said a fairy.

'Yes,' said Regio. 'It would explain a lot if her magic was literally made for water riding.'

A chuckle came from the back, and the crowd parted around a worn, aging man, arms folded across his chest. He was tall and stocky, with brown curly hair and a thick mustache peppered with white, but his round face was kind, and his eyes crinkled as he laughed.

He met Storm's gaze. 'Only one line remains,' said the man. 'Me and my niece, although Alba is no longer here, and I am old, my magic not what it once was.'

Some of the group tried to leave after that, edging towards the tunnels with a panicked look in their eyes. They'd all seen what could happen when riders fell in the lake, and none of them wanted to be next in line to have their arms and legs torn from their torsos. Axus put a stop to their retreat, although his face had also turned ashen, his eyes darting to his son at regular intervals.

'The plan,' said Storm—for what could she do but continue?—'is to lure a Scarani up from the deep, then ride it to the shore. Once we have grounded the beast, we will draw its life magic, then remove its scales.'

'How big are these … Scarani?' said the female pixie.

'Big,' said Storm.

'How big?' she persisted.

Storm's eyes stretched across the cavern. 'The old ones—the kind we need—will stretch almost from one side of the lake to the other.'

Everyone went quiet.

'And they're smart,' said Storm, 'with speed enhanced by magic.'

'Why are the Children in need of appeasement anyway?' said the pixie.

Storm raised an eyebrow at Axus.

'It matters not,' he said.

'Come on,' said one of the cockier fae. 'If you want us to risk our necks, you could at least tell us why!' He was young, with outlandish good looks, and Storm scowled hard in his direction.

'Axus?' Storm said. She turned to face the wall, silently asking the Gods what in the Seven Hells Isa was playing at up here. What had she been teaching them? Or, more to the point, not teaching them ...

'I ... well ...' said Axus.

Storm spun back around, her brow furrowed.

'I ... am not at liberty to say,' said Axus, then clamped his mouth shut and folded his arms across his chest.

'You don't know?' said Storm.

'I know,' he snarled, 'but I must consult with Isa before saying more.'

Storm paced for a moment, lining up her thoughts. The Fae'ch were in much worse shape than she'd known. Sure, the long-lives of the deep loved nothing more than to mock Isa and criticize her decisions, but Storm had never imagined for a moment she was mismanaging their people to such a dangerous extent. What else was Isa keeping from them?

She took a breath. If Isa wouldn't tell them, Storm would. 'Everything in our world must exist in balance,' she said. 'That much should be obvious ... common sense ... and we are not the oldest, scariest, most powerful magical beings in existence. The fae have always longed to be such—some more deeply than others—but longing does not make it so.

'The Children of the Lake, and many other magical beings under the mountain, were already here when our kind fled the Five Kingdoms. Our magic was weakening, and the human Kings pressed their advantage, forcing us to the only safe place we could find, but we were invaders, no choice but to beg for space under the mountain that already belonged to others.'

Storm paced as she talked, looking into their faces, showing them she spoke the truth. 'The beings already here had power that surpassed our own. They could have snuffed us out, but with careful negotiation, we

132

came to an agreement. Some retreated to live deeper under the mountain, others went to the depths of the lake, but the Children refused to abandon the upper levels.'

'Why?' said Regio, his eyes shining with intrigue.

'This is their home,' said Storm. 'They were here first, and we are here at their mercy, safe only so long as we give them what they need.'

'Magic,' said Veau.

Storm nodded. 'Magic. Not too much, and not too little. Just enough.'

Regio had the decency to look guilty about feeding the Children dragon scales. Axus didn't.

'So we must find a source of magic that provides just that,' said Storm.

'What will happen if we fail?' asked Regio.

Storm's eyebrows lifted, and she appraised the group anew. 'If I were you, weak as you are, I'd pray I never found out.'

Storm worked them for hours, doing drills with the smaller serpent-like beasts that lived at the shallow end of the lake. They were feared by these imposters who called themselves water riders, although in truth, they were nothing compared to the monster they must find.

'We will meet again tomorrow,' said Storm, when they were sweaty and exhausted, and one fairy had come close to losing an arm. 'At dawn.'

They filed out, grumbling to one other, saying they wished they hadn't answered the call. Veau was the only one to hang back.

'You wanted to speak with me?' he said. He had never proclaimed himself a water rider, but he'd watched and learned.

'Why did you want to speak with Axus earlier?' said Storm. A human with little magic under the mountain was strange enough, but seeking out a senior fae showed audacity … or leverage.

Veau's forehead furrowed, then he shook his head and waved his hand. 'My sister came to the mountain, seeking the dragon egg under Fae'ch protection.'

'Did she indeed …'

'Isa agreed to show it to her, but it was missing.'

'Missing?' said Storm.

'I was there. I saw the whole thing. They're stoking rumors that Fyia stole the egg, but she didn't. It wasn't there.'

A missing egg … could it be the dragons would truly return? Could that be the source of the disturbance? 'I want to learn about your sister.'

Veau's face set hard.

'Fear not, it's nothing bad. I'm … intrigued by her. I believe she intends to welcome the magical back to her lands, and I want to know if it's a call I should answer.'

Veau's jaw literally dropped, and Storm laughed.

'It can't be so much of a surprise,' said Storm. 'Life under the mountain is hardly ideal.'

'Especially for you,' said Veau, then immediately looked sheepish.

'Especially for anyone,' she parried. 'So, tell me, is your sister a queen worthy of the name?'

'Yes,' said Veau, without hesitation. 'My sister is … I don't know. She's infuriating most of the time, and stubborn, and once she gets an idea in her head, there's no reasoning with her.'

'Like conquering five kingdoms?' Storm said with a chuckle.

'Like bringing back the dragons,' he said darkly.

Storm stilled for a moment, taking him in. 'You think it a foolish quest?'

Veau shook his head. 'No. I think if anyone can do it, it will be her, but …'

He trailed off as footsteps approached, and Gabriel appeared through a tunnel. 'This is Veau,' said Storm. 'The Queen's brother. Also fire-touched, in case you hadn't noticed the scales across his face.'

Veau frowned.

'Don't mind her,' said Gabriel. 'She's insensitive.'

Storm gave a half smile just as Isa appeared in front of Gabriel, materializing in a whirl of smoke. She laid a hand on his chest, and Storm clenched her teeth.

'Where have you been?' said Isa, her voice distant, not fully with them.

'I've been busy,' said Gabriel. Storm suspected he'd mostly been busy avoiding her.

'Doing what?' said Isa, the words a dangerous purr.

'Asking around in the deep for food we can use for the Children,' said Gabriel. Storm conceded that might be true.

An awkward silence descended as Isa's focus left them, presumably watching some other part of the mountain with her magic.

Veau stepped closer, waiting for Isa to return before saying, 'Have you found the dragon egg?'

Isa's eyes snapped to Veau. 'Quiet,' she hissed.

'It's missing?' said Gabriel.

'Maybe you should ask your sister,' said Isa.

'She took it?' said Gabriel.

'No,' Veau said firmly. 'Axus took Fyia to the egg, but it was missing. I saw the whole thing with my own eyes.'

Veau had spirit, and Storm found herself beginning to like him. 'Even so,' said Storm, 'that's the least of your worries. The Children are nervous. They …'

'You will placate them,' said Isa. She shifted, so they were face to face, her eyes full of menace.

'As you wish, leader,' said Storm, with a mock bow, 'but to placate them, I need water riders, and you have all but extinguished their magic from our kind. Where is the one they call Alba?'

Isa clenched her jaw. 'She has gone to learn about the new Queen.'

The sound of wings drew their attention, unusual under the mountain, as wings were generally kept hidden, for some senseless etiquette-based reason Isa had invented.

Regio's form ejected from the tunnel with terrific speed. 'Something's happened to the Kraken Emperor!' he said, the words rushing out in a jumble. 'Alba and my brother sent word. The Queen has …'

Regio's mouth froze, and then he fell from the sky, landing hard. His eyes went wide with terror, his hands clutching his throat.

'Isa …' said Gabriel, stepping forward.

Isa held Gabriel's gaze, then swiped her hand through the air. Regio gasped, sucking breath into his lungs.

Isa sneered as a cloud of smoke wrapped around her. She all but disappeared, only her head remaining as she fixed her eyes on Veau, then turned to Gabriel. 'I see you've found your son, my love.'

Isa disappeared entirely, but Gabriel didn't notice. His eyes turned to Veau, and his stomach bottomed out, guilt and shame filling him.

'You're his son?' said Storm, looking to Veau for confirmation.

Veau didn't answer, his eyes fixed on Gabriel, his face pale.

'We'll leave you two alone,' said Storm, motioning to Regio. 'Find me when you're done. I have questions, and I want answers.'

They left, and Gabriel and Veau just stood there, watching each other for a beat, two, three.

'I thought the King of Starlight was my father,' said Veau, his words uncertain.

'Apparently not,' said Gabriel. 'If it's any consolation, I only found out yesterday I had a son, and Isa didn't tell me who you were.'

'Then it's a surprise for both of us.'

Gabriel nodded, not sure what to say. 'I'm sorry,' was all he could manage.

'For what?' said Veau. 'Impregnating my mother?'

'I … well …' Gabriel was off kilter. It felt like the whole place might be spinning, like the water in the lake might spill out at any moment.

'Did you love her?' said Veau.

'No,' said Gabriel, fervently, then realized Veau might have been hoping for a different answer. 'I'm sure your mother is a wonderful woman,' he added, 'but I barely knew her.'

Veau snorted. 'My mother is anything but wonderful … but, if you didn't know her … why?'

'Isa,' said Gabriel.

'Oh.'

'She was angry her efforts to get with child were not bearing fruit, and then your mother came to the mountain. I believe she intended to find a magical

137

father for her child, and Isa wanted to punish me, so …'

'So she forced you?' said Veau, his face falling.

Shit. Maybe he shouldn't have said that. But it was the truth. 'Yes, she forced me, but that has no bearing on how I think about you … or how you should think about yourself. You can hardly be judged because of the actions of Isa and your mother … and me.'

'I'm sorry,' said Veau, his features pensive. 'For both our sakes.'

Silence descended as their new roles settled on their shoulders.

'Lucky you didn't inherit my wings,' said Gabriel. 'Unless you're hiding them with magic …'

'No,' said Veau, shaking his head. 'I have only weak, erratic magic. That, and the scales across my face.'

'Well, you didn't get those from me,' said Gabriel, 'although your ears have a very slight point. I think we can attribute those to your fae blood.'

'It finally makes sense why Isa agreed to let me live under the mountain,' said Veau. 'For you. Because she loves you.'

Gabriel laughed. 'That woman doesn't know how to love. She brought you here to torment me, or use you as a hostage.'

'Rumor says Isa is head over heels in love with you …'

'What she feels isn't love, despite what she may believe,' said Gabriel. 'She cares only for power and control. She's desperate to keep her place as leader of our kind, but fears the long-lives in the deep might get rebellious ideas … or up and leave. Now your sister's welcoming us back to her lands, Isa walks a precarious line.'

'You would leave?' said Veau. 'I never really believed any of the Fae'ch would take up Fyia's offer.'

'Why not? You think we enjoy living under this damned mountain?'

Veau thought for a moment. 'Honestly, yes,' he said. 'That's how it looks from the outside, but maybe that's because Isa allows no one in.'

'Come,' said Gabriel, 'let us go to Storm; she wishes to know more about your sister.'

'Half-sister,' said Veau. 'Unless …'

'No,' said Gabriel. 'It happened only once.'

Veau huffed out a laugh. 'People in the Five Kingdoms made such a fuss when I gave my throne to Fyia, and it turns out she was the rightful heir all along.'

'You're still the son of the Queen of Starlight,' said Gabriel. 'Magic- and fire-touched. That's not nothing.'

Veau laughed again. 'I hardly think my paltry magic warrants the title.'

'It is strong for a human, is it not?'

Veau shrugged. 'It's hard to say. Until Fyia took over, anyone with even a hint of magic hid their talent for fear of persecution, or death.'

'We will test it,' said Gabriel. 'But first, we will speak with Storm.'

⁕————•◆►··◄◆•————•

Gabriel led his son into the depths of the mountain, ignoring Veau's tense features and hesitant steps. If Veau were here alone, he would be right to be worried, but with Gabriel, and at this level, there wasn't much to fear … well, aside from Storm.

They entered the cave Gabriel and Storm shared, and Storm threw out her arm with a shriek, hurling a barrage of magic directly at Veau. Gabriel's heart leapt, but his son reacted, ducking just in time.

'His magic's not as bad as I've heard,' Storm said with a shrug.

'Storm,' Gabriel growled, his heart still racing.

Storm smiled sweetly. 'It was the only way to test his reflexes.'

Gabriel shook his head, but Veau's eyes were wide with wonder. 'How do you mean, *it's not as bad as you've heard*?' he said.

Storm's smile broadened. 'Maybe you got lucky,' she said. 'I'll have to test you some more, but on the surface, it would appear your magic detected the threat and responded.'

Storm led Veau and Gabriel to the low couches arranged around a table made of bones.

'Not everyone under the mountain can do that,' said Gabriel, sitting next to Storm.

'Especially as Isa is letting certain types of magic die out,' said Storm.

'She is?' said Veau, leaning forward, his arms on his knees.

Storm leaned back in her seat. 'There are no water riders. Only the old man, Pips, and his niece, Alba.'

'You really think she did that on purpose?' said Veau.

'No,' said Gabriel, at the same time as Storm said, 'Yes.'

Gabriel scowled at her. 'You have no way of knowing that.'

'Either she did it on purpose,' said Storm, 'or she realized and did nothing about it. Or worst of all, she didn't know. And if she didn't know, then what else has she missed?'

Gabriel couldn't deny the logic, although Isa had a lot on her plate. It was possible she knew and decided it wasn't worth bothering about, for whatever misguided reason.

'She's blaming my sister for the missing dragon egg,' said Veau, 'and Fyia had nothing to do with it. And why was Isa suddenly happy to show Fyia the egg at all?'

'The Children are unhappy,' said Storm. 'Isa's probably terrified. Or maybe she *couldn't* do anything about the dwindling magic of the water riders. Magic has continued to weaken since the dragons fled, after all.'

'Who knows?' said Gabriel. 'Isa keeps her cards close to her chest.'

'Not with you,' said Storm. 'You could find out.'

Gabriel shuddered. 'I'm not so sure …'

Storm held his gaze for a moment, then shook her head as if to clear it. 'Well, anyway, tell me what your sister wants out of all this?' she said, pinning Veau with razor eyes.

Veau smiled. 'She wants to bring back the dragons.'

'But, why?'

'She believes the legends … that she can thaw the north and bring prosperity to all. And she wants to live in harmony with the magical, and free the persecuted, and allow women to live as equals with men.'

'She's an idealist,' said Storm.

'Many call her that,' said Veau. 'They say it like it's a bad thing, but it's not. She wants to change the ways of the world, and so far, she's done everything they said she couldn't.'

'She's not scared the magic-folk will steal her power?'

'She has more faith in your kind than that.'

'Our kind,' said Storm.

141

Veau tipped his head to the side, as though only just realizing he was Fae'ch.

'Should we go to her side?' said Storm. 'Would you, if you could control your power?'

'You're truly considering it?'

'Aren't you?' said Storm.

Veau laughed. 'I only just got here.'

'And Isa won't let you go,' said Gabriel.

'Because she thinks she can use me to control you?' said Veau.

Gabriel inclined his head. 'It's certainly possible she would use you in that way.'

'What he means to say is, if it suited Isa's purposes, she wouldn't hesitate,' said Storm.

'Why can't Isa deal with the Children of the Lake?' said Veau. 'I thought she was ancient and all powerful … or that's what everyone upstairs seems to think. And even those of you living down here still answer to her, do you not?'

Storm shook her head. 'Isa only leads because in a moment of stupidity, we allowed her to.'

'But … why?'

It was Storm's story to tell, unlikely as she was to tell it.

'More importantly,' said Storm, 'if your sister brings back the dragons, the Children will leave the lake and sap the magic from everything they can find.'

Veau paled.

'And then they'll want more, for that is their nature.'

'Why would they do that?' Veau whispered. His fingers clutched the edge of his seat, his knuckles white.

'Because magic is their food,' said Storm, 'and to fell a dragon is their highest prize. But it matters not, for if we can't placate them soon, and bring them safely down from their dragon scale high, they will come out of the lake anyway and eat us all alive.'

Veau's mouth fell open.

'Storm …' said Gabriel, the word a warning. None of this was Veau's fault, and he didn't know he'd touched a nerve. There was no need for her to play with him … to confuse and terrify.

'Now,' said Storm, 'tell me, what does your sister want with the Kraken Emperor?'

Veau stayed silent for many long moments. 'You seem unconcerned about being eaten,' he said.

Storm shrugged. 'If your sister wants magic back in the world, get used to threats to your existence, but if I am to leave this place and go to her side, I must understand her. So, why would she care about the Emperor?'

'How would I know?' said Veau. 'I've been under the mountain.'

'Guess,' said Storm.

'He got in her way … or tried to force her into marriage,' he said. 'My parents arranged a marriage between Fyia and the Emperor years ago. Fyia ran away rather than marry him. She won't be forced into anything, and especially not that.'

'Wise woman,' said Storm.

'Why isn't Isa placating the Children herself?' said Veau, returning to the line of questioning Storm had tried to deflect him from. A prickle of pride took hold in Gabriel's chest, shocking him.

Storm laughed. 'The Children hate her. They would eat her alive if she ever tried.'

'But they like you?' said Veau. 'Why?'

'Because I'm *special*,' said Storm, widening her eyes as she said the word.

'Special how?'

Storm was enjoying the tussle, so she rewarded him with a morsel. 'I helped them when no one else would. Many hundreds of years ago.'

* * *

Veau returned to his own quarters—wherever they were—and Gabriel rounded on Storm, flying at her and pinning her to the wall. 'You could have hurt him,' he said, his hands on her shoulders, his head hovering above hers.

'Lucky for him, his reflexes are good,' said Storm, tipping her head back and looking up into his eyes.

He lowered his lips and captured her mouth, the kiss punishing. He nipped and kissed her as his hands slid to her neck, and she moaned, sliding her hands over his backside, holding him against her.

Gabriel pulled away and rested his forehead against hers. 'Be careful around Isa,' he said softly. 'I know you hate her, but she's a malicious witch, and her back is against the wall. She might lash out.'

'She needs me more than I need her,' said Storm, sliding a finger along the seam of his wing.

Gabriel shuddered. 'She could find a way to pin you under this mountain ...'

She tugged on a feather, and Gabriel winced. 'I'd happily live another five hundred years down here if it meant screwing with her plans.'

'In another delusion?'

'Even better,' she said, but they both knew it was a lie. Her delusion had been a warped reconstruction of reality, and Storm had been as unhappy there as she was under Isa's control.

Gabriel took hold of her chin, pulling it up so he could look down into her eyes. 'Never run away from me again,' he said. 'When you left, I didn't know if I'd get you back, and it nearly killed me.'

'You should have had more faith in your abilities,' she said with a coy smile.

'Don't joke,' he said, resting his forehead against hers. 'I mean it ... please.'

'I won't,' she said, 'probably ... Because I'm getting out of here.'

Gabriel pushed a stand of hair back off her face. 'If you leave, the Children will kill everyone under the mountain ...'

She grabbed his hand, stilling his movement, and her expression turned serious. 'They're going to do that anyway,' she said. 'I can only placate them for so long ... the disturbance is too great, and Isa's hiding, doing nothing at all.'

Gabriel stilled. 'You're sure? Even if the dragons never return?'

Storm nodded. 'It's inevitable. Whatever's coming is too big to stop.'

'We need to tell Isa.'

'No,' said Storm. '*You* need to tell Isa. I need to buy us time with the Children.'

'And if she doesn't believe me?'

'Then many of our kind will die—people we can't afford to lose—and it'll happen even sooner if I can't trap a monster from the deep.'

'Training was bad?'

'Terrible,' said Storm. Images of her trainees falling from baby serpents flashed across her mind. 'None of them have water magic, so nothing's intuitive. The winged Fae'ch want to use their wings, refusing to feel the monster under their feet ... the pulse of water all around.'

'What about the old man, Pips?' said Gabriel.

Storm huffed out a laugh. 'He waited two minutes for me to turn my back, then disappeared. When I asked Axus where he'd gone, he told me he's an adventurer and has left the mountain.'

'To go where?'

Storm shrugged. 'Axus didn't know.'

'Fuck.'

'Quite,' said Storm. 'And who is Regio's brother?'

'What?'

'Regio said he'd received word from the water rider Alba, and his brother. Isa didn't mention the brother when she told us Alba had gone to spy on the Queen …'

Gabriel shrugged. 'I don't know.'

Storm slid her hands up into his hair and went up on her tiptoes. 'Then I shall have to find out.' She kissed him again, but a knock sounded on the wooden door. Storm waved her hand to pull it open, the door peeling back to reveal Michael's winged form.

'Am I interrupting?'

'Yes,' said Storm.

'Glad to hear it,' said Michael, striding into the room with a cruel smile on his lips. 'But I come bearing gifts.' He held up a vial filled with liquid the color of aquamarine and a wooden bowl filled with white powder.

'You ground the crystals from Fairy Land?' said Gabriel.

'I did,' said Michael, 'and convinced the bad-tempered old chemists to give me this.' He shook the vial and raised his eyebrows salaciously.

'Aqua bloom?' said Storm.

'Exactly,' said Michael.

'Good,' said Storm.

The chemists made the potion from rare algae blooms that grew deep in the mountain.

'They said the algae is particularly active right now,' said Michael, 'meaning they were surprisingly happy to hand it over.'

'Maybe the algae can feel the disturbance in the air, too,' said Storm.

'Shall we?' said Michael. He took his treasures to the bone table and sank to his knees before it.

'Let me,' said Storm. She followed him, then snagged the vial from his hand.

'Why, of course,' Michael said sarcastically.

Storm dropped to her knees as she pulled the stopper from the vial, then carefully tipped three drops into the bowl. The drops sat atop the powder as Storm stoppered the vial then picked up the bowl. She carefully tipped it first one way and then the other, edging the drops across the powder. The powder slowly sucked up the liquid, turning turquoise then solidifying, crystalizing before their eyes.

Michael handed Storm a copper spatula, and she carefully lifted the newly formed crystal, placing it on a glass plate Michael had rustled up from nowhere.

Storm repeated the process until she had five large, perfectly straight crystals, then put down her tools, sighing deeply.

'Those should buy us some time at least,' said Michael.

'Not long,' said Storm. 'The aqua bloom will appeal to the Children, but only because they haven't had it in a while. It contains little magic.'

Michael shrugged. 'It was all I could get anyone to hand over …'

'They're miserable old codgers,' said Storm. 'They're probably hoarding; preparing their escape.'

'Why?' said Michael, drawing out the word in a child-like way.

'Because the Children are going to eat us all alive,' said Gabriel, cheerily.

Michael looked from Gabriel to Storm and back again. 'Shit,' he said. 'You're serious!'

Storm nodded. 'Spread the word, but do so quietly, lest our illustrious leader nip our preparations in the bud.'

Chapter Eleven

STORM STRODE TOWARDS THE lake with her shoulders back, her head held high. Yesterday had been a worrying start, but she was sure today they'd make progress. However, the crowd next to the lake was half the size of the day before, and her chest constricted at the sight. Even Veau was missing.

'The others are too cowardly to return?' she said, skimming the rag-tag faces.

'Apparently,' said Regio, with a cocky smile.

Storm resisted the temptation to roll her eyes. 'Seeing as yesterday was so disappointing,' she said, 'we'll try something different today.'

The group's eyes were glued to her, following her every move as she paced back and forth. She nodded to Axus, who carried a small cloth sack. He threw it to her, and she pulled it open and tipped out the contents, letting the blindfolds within fall to the floor.

'The beasts we need reside out there, in the dark,' said Storm. 'The chase to catch them will span a vast area, and it will be impossible to provide light at all times, so we will train in the darkness.'

Their faces—already betraying their nerves—turned sheet white.

'Fret not,' said Storm, 'you will practice first on dry land. Partner up and navigate over the rocks and around the water's edge with blindfolds over your eyes. If you have wings, do not use them. Use your ears, and nose, and all your senses. Learn quickly, for I will return within a single turn of the clock.'

Their grumbling followed Storm as she skirted the lake, heading for the Children. She could only imagine how they would grumble when they discovered they would have to leave their precious mountain to avoid being eaten alive.

Storm entered the cave, and the Children popped into the air to greet her. They seemed perkier than before, less hostile; a good sign.

'Good morning,' said Storm. She dug her hand into her pocket and wrapped her fingers around the turquoise crystals. 'Did you enjoy the show yesterday?'

'You call that a show?' said the oldest of the Children, but the voice had a teasing edge.

'A comedy, perhaps,' Storm conceded, 'but they will improve, and then you shall have a magnificent gift.'

'Hmm,' said another, 'and in the meantime?'

Storm smiled. 'I have not come to my friends empty handed,' she said. She pulled out the crystals and held them in her open palm, showing them her offering.

They began to buzz, excitement filling the air, and Storm grinned. 'I'm glad you like them.'

'It has been a long time,' said one. It darted forward and rolled across a crystal. The crystal disappeared, and the Child shone more brightly.

The others followed suit, until Storm's hand was empty, and the Children were back in the lake.

'A pleasant surprise,' said the oldest, 'but it will not keep us satisfied for long.'

'Of course, my friend,' said Storm. 'Soon I shall provide a more nutritious meal.'

'Time will tell ...'

The words rang through Storm's mind as she returned to training, which was, if possible, even worse than the day before. Regio tripped over a stone, and a fairy took two full steps into the water. *Shit.*

'Why can't the Children just catch a lake monster for themselves?' said the female pixie. She was reclining on a stone, watching as a dwarf banged into the rocks.

'They've eaten all the lake creatures with accessible magic,' said Storm. 'They did so soon after they agreed to live in the lake. They have relied upon us to provide them with ample food ever since. They are lazy by nature, so the arrangement suits them well enough.

'After we capture a suitable monster, we must extract the magic from its scales and mix it with a crystal powder before feeding it to the Children.'

'*If* we capture a lake monster, and don't all die first,' said a fairy.

Storm balled her fists. How had she ended up here? Training those with no clue about anything, having responsibilities, dealing with the inevitable backchat of subordinates. This was the reason she and Gabriel had handed power to Isa, and had been glad to do so ... or at least part of the reason.

'You're right,' said Storm, her tone overly bright. 'You need to practice. Do that for the rest of the day. I will return at dawn to assess your progress.'

Storm was climbing the walls by the time Gabriel appeared in their rooms. 'It's a disaster,' she said, before he'd even closed the door.

'That bad?'

'Worse.'

'Same.'

'Fuck.'

'I told Isa it was only a matter of time before the Children leave the lake, but she didn't believe me. She thinks you're trying to drive a wedge between her and I … that you're lying.'

'A wedge?' laughed Storm. 'Does she not realize there's already an entire canyon between you, and it has nothing to do with me?'

'I saw Veau,' said Gabriel, 'to train him.'

'At least that explains why he wasn't at the lake.'

'He's got potential,' said Gabriel, pouring them both a drink from an aged, misshapen glass bottle.

Storm accepted her glass and took a long sip. 'Gods, this stuff is disgusting.'

'Yes,' agreed Gabriel, 'but it numbs the pain.'

She took another swig, then started pacing, but walking back and forth only wound her frustration tighter, until she shrieked. 'Why did we let her lead?'

'Because we were trying to be nice, we don't care for power, and we are lazy.'

'And she knows my secret,' said Storm, bitterly.

'That too.' Gabriel took another sip, then cast his glass aside.

Storm's feet rooted to the spot as he approached, and she downed her own drink, then used magic to send her glass to the table. But the liquor was already making her head swim, and she missed. The glass tumbled to the floor, the smash reverberating around them.

Gabriel lowered his head to her neck and sank his teeth into her flesh, hard enough to ease her frustration, yet soft enough to send a bolt of desire to her core. 'Again,' she said, when he tried to pull back, her hand in his hair, not letting him go.

He did it again, this time harder, and she gasped at the pain. She lifted her leg, and Gabriel caught it behind the knee, then hoisted her against him.

'Again,' she whispered. He moved to the other side, so he could more easily grind his hips against her, then he pressed his lips to her neck and sucked. Storm moaned, her knees going weak.

Storm's head whirled, barely knowing which way was up, as Gabriel continued his assault on her neck. She rubbed against the bulge in his breeches, but it wasn't enough, so she took a step back, trying to pull him towards the bed.

He picked her up and spread his wings, lifting them off the ground in one swift sweep. She thrust her fingers into his feathers, one hand on each side, and they plummeted onto the bed. Gabriel's weight landed hard on top of Storm, just as she'd wanted, and as he tried to lift himself off her, she dug her hands into his wings once more, hitting the spots she knew would make him squirm.

A spasm gripped Gabriel, and he bucked, the movement slamming his body against Storm's. 'Yes,' she breathed.

'Storm, I don't want to hurt you.'

'But I want it …' She caressed his wings, one hand tracing where his wing joined his shoulder, the other skirting the ridge at the top.

'Storm,' he groaned.

She grasped a handful of feathers and tugged with enough force to make him buck once more. She tugged again and again, and he pulsed his hips in time with her fingers, her pulls a little gentler than the first, but still edged with pain.

'*Warrior* ...' he gasped.

'The Gods can't help you,' she whispered in his ear. She pulled his head to hers, and he kissed her with deep, rhythmic movements that made her eyes roll back in her head.

'Clothes,' said Storm. But she didn't want to let him go, tipping her hips as she said the word, seeking friction.

Gabriel pulled away, and they made short work of their clothing. Then he settled back atop her, lining himself up with her entrance as she spread her legs.

She pulled on his feathers once more, and he pushed inside her with a sharp exhale, his hips moving wildly as she held his feathers hostage. 'Storm,' he groaned, sliding his hands under her behind, lifting her hips off the bed.

'Mmmm,' she said, then pushed her hand between them, finding his balls.

Gabriel choked, and Storm laughed.

He became a blur of movement, pulling out, turning her onto her front, then pinning her with his weight. He entered her, his chest pressed to her back, and slid a hand under her hips. He found the spot that made her moan, bringing her to the brink twice before finally allowing her to convulse around him. She clawed at the bedding as spasms wracked her body, the waves rolling through her as Gabriel groaned, then stilled, then collapsed on top of her, his wings fanning out across the bed.

Storm led training for days on end with little progress. It was taking so long, Storm feared the Children would lose patience before the riders were ready ... if they would ever be ready.

She'd been feeding the Children crystals of aqua bloom, which still delighted them, but eventually, that delight would turn sour. The pressure sat in Storm's gut like a weight.

At least Gabriel had been making progress with Veau, whose magic was now almost entirely under control, and, although weak by fae standards, was impressive for a human.

Gabriel joined Storm in the shadows, where she stood watching the trainees as they rode the lesser monsters. He wrapped his arms around her waist, pulling her back against him, and Storm closed her eyes, letting herself enjoy the simple pleasure, but only for a moment.

'Have you found a knife?' she asked, stroking his arm.

'No,' said Gabriel. 'None of the long-lives have one. Or if they do, they're not admitting it.'

'What do you need?' said Regio, appearing out of the tunnel near where they stood. 'Sorry,' he added sheepishly. 'I couldn't help but overhear.'

'You're late,' said Storm.

'Yes, I had to help ... well, I'm sorry. But whatever you need, I might know people ...'

'How?' said Storm. She held his overly eager eyes for a beat, then turned back to watch the trainees, lest she need to stage a rescue.

'Uh ...' said Regio. His eyes found his father, who sat on the other side of the lake. 'I have an *in* with the Black Guild, but if my father ever found out ...'

'We need a Luscini knife,' said Storm. 'Do you know what that is?'

'No,' said Regio, with a beaming smile, 'but I'd be happy to find out.'

Storm turned her head to look at him again. 'Why so enthusiastic?' she asked, cocking a suggestive eyebrow, a teasing smile pulling at her lips.

'No reason,' said Regio, but he couldn't dampen his grin.

Storm laughed, his mood contagious. 'Off you … actually, before you go find whoever's done this to you.'

'Yes?'

'Why did Isa send your brother with the water rider?'

Regio went still, his eyes flicking nervously from Storm to Gabriel, then to his father. 'Leo's …'

When no further words followed, Storm prompted, 'Yes?'

Regio shifted uncomfortably. 'Leo is … well …' He stole another quick glance at Gabriel. 'He's …' Regio wrung his hands. 'I really shouldn't say.'

All humor left Storm's face, her patience running thin. 'It would be a shame for your *in* with the Black Guild to get back to Daddy …' she said. 'Is Axus Leo's father too?'

Regio's features turned as bitter as the words that followed. 'We share the same father, but different mothers.'

'And …' said Storm, tempted to jab him with her magic.

Regio cast a concerned look towards Gabriel. 'I assumed you knew.'

'Knew what?' said Gabriel, but Storm's blood ran cold.

Regio squared his shoulders. 'Leo is Isa's son.'

Gabriel sucked in a breath, as though he'd taken an unexpected punch to the stomach.

Storm dismissed Regio with a nod, and he fled.

She slipped her hand into Gabriel's, holding tight. It wasn't as though Gabriel would care about Isa having a child with another, but the shock of it ... that Isa had kept knowledge of her child from Gabriel, while making Gabriel perform unspeakable acts, while pretending all she wanted in the world was a child ...

They stood watching the trainees in silence for a whole turn of the clock, Gabriel neither moving a muscle nor saying a word. Storm was about to call the trainees in, to put an end to their miserable display and take Gabriel back to their cave, when Pips appeared at the tunnel's entrance.

Storm pushed away from Gabriel. 'Pips?' she said. 'Where have you been?'

Pips held out a bag and wiggled it back and forth. 'See for yourself,' he said with a wink.

Storm took in his disheveled appearance, the gash across his cheek, and the way he was favoring one leg, then snatched up the bag and yanked it open, gasping when she saw what it contained.

'You're welcome,' said Pips, then limped off to join the others. 'Let me show you young'ens how it's done!' he said. He pulled a tether from his pocket, then jumped atop a cresting monster.

Storm looked up at Gabriel. 'Bait,' she said.

'And Sulu-Weed,' he replied.

'By the Gods,' said Storm. 'Maybe we can do this after all.'

'This is Sulu-Weed,' Storm told the trainees the following morning. She held up the green, curly weed, treating it with the utmost care. 'It is extremely rare, and grows only in the deepest, darkest waters of the Kingdom of Starlight.'

'What's it for?' asked Regio, rolling an apple from one hand to the other.

'Long ago,' said Storm, 'water riders were called upon to protect their people against all manner of creatures. So many monsters lurked in rivers and lakes, and in the shallows of the seas, there weren't enough water riders to keep up with demand.

'But a group of diving anglers found a weed they'd never seen before at the bottom of a lake. They ate it, and could *feel* the water, and sense the water creatures in a way they couldn't before.'

'It turns you into a water rider?' said Regio, leaning forward.

'It allows you to imitate one for a time,' said Storm, 'until the effects wear off.'

'At which point, you'll experience the worst hangover of your life!' said Pips, happily. 'Not that I'd know, but it'll last three days if rumors can be believed.'

'Wonderful,' said Regio, leaning back.

'We have enough weed for a dry run and two tries,' said Storm. 'We'll spread the attempts out to allow time for recovery.'

'If we don't get eaten first,' said Regio.

'If you don't get eaten first,' Storm agreed, 'but this stuff,' she held up the bag, 'improves your chances no end.'

The trainees had dwindled to a group of only four—Regio, Axus, Veau, and Pips—and they did not look impressed, but then, they were covered in scrapes and bruises, and had endured endless near misses.

It wasn't the group Storm would have selected, but they were gutsy, and that was all she could ask. At least aside from Axus, who did little but watch. Pips was the only one with any real skill, but what Regio lacked in ability, he made up for in confidence, and Veau was a quick study.

'Pips also found bait,' said Storm, smiling at the old man. 'I've been meaning to ask, where did you find them?'

'Find what?' said Regio, trying to peer into the bag Storm held in her hand.

Storm chuckled. 'They're not in here,' she said.

'Bones,' said Pips, 'of an extinct fish. I heard tell several years ago of some atop the pink cliffs of Starlight, although I never had cause to go looking. It was a long journey, first to the mountains in the east for the weed, then to the coast in the west for the bones, but we need both if we are to stand any chance at all.'

'The bones were at the top of the cliffs?' said Regio, his face screwed up in confusion. 'The fish could climb?'

Pips laughed. 'No. The water was once higher, and land shifts about. I've seen seashells atop mountains.'

'And they were just lying there?' said Regio.

'Apparently,' said Pips. 'A local merchant collected every last one he could find. No one was interested, but he knew one day a customer would come looking.'

'And the monsters of the deep want *bones*?' said Veau.

'These bones, yes,' said Storm. 'They contain Calcita, something the monsters need but rarely get. Without it, they'll eventually die, although they last several hundred years first. It's found in the bones of some magic folk too … you must have noticed when dwarves ride the monsters, more creatures come to the surface?'

'Dwarves rarely ride,' said Regio. 'I thought it was because they were short.'

Storm sent him a dirty look. 'Let's get to it,' she said. She carefully ripped small sections of weed and handed it around. 'Chew five times, then swallow every bit.'

They all took a piece, aside from Pips and Storm, whose magic needed no enhancement.

As the others headed to the water's edge, ready to be carried out to the darkness for their dry run, Regio hung back. 'I've got a lead on a Luscini knife,' he said quietly. 'The Black Guild are working on it, but they want to know what it's for?'

'Your girlfriend asked, and it made you look bad when you didn't know?' Storm joked. Regio's cheeks reddened, and Storm laughed. 'It's for cutting the scales from the monster in a way that preserves their magic.'

'Oh,' said Regio. 'I guess that makes sense.'

Storm nodded, then grabbed Gabriel's arm, pulling him close as they followed Regio to the water. 'The Children are restless,' she said, 'they were short with me this morning, and I can feel it in the air. Be careful.'

Gabriel kissed her cheek, then moved to Pips' side and lifted him off the ground. Regio carried Veau, and the others flew under their own steam as they ventured into the dark, Storm leading the way.

'How come you can fly but have no wings?' Regio asked Storm.

Storm took a deep breath. 'Magic,' she said, her tone making it clear she would give nothing else away.

Storm's heart raced as they flew further and further from safety. The fae had excellent eyesight, even in the gloom, and they had the enhancements offered by the Sulu-Weed, but she felt as though she rode a skittish horse, like she might be thrown at any moment.

They flew in silence; the tense kind reserved for fear of the unknown. For even if Gabriel and Storm had seen monsters of the type they sought before, they had never been foolhardy enough to approach them with a band of amateurs.

When Storm deemed they'd flown far enough, she pulled out the smallest of the fish bones—no bigger than a fingernail—and dropped it into the water.

The water immediately shuddered and shook, small fountains shooting up then falling back, and Storm's brow furrowed. The Children had followed them, and this was their work.

'Steady, my old friends,' Storm said aloud. 'We hunt for you; allow us that honor.'

The water stilled a moment, then Pips shouted, 'One's coming! I can feel it!'

Storm could feel it too, an enormous weight gliding upwards through the cool.

'More than one,' said Pips, his voice urgent. 'They're … wait … they're everywhere!'

'Up!' cried Storm.

They rose as one towards the ceiling of the great cavern, but Storm feared it was not high enough. The monsters had been growing for hundreds of years, picking off the smaller beasts and fish of the lake. What if they could reach the ceiling? And for them to be this eager … she wondered just how long it been since they'd last consumed Calcita.

A wave rose suddenly out of the water, knocking Axus out of the sky.

'Dad!' Regio screamed. He made a dive towards the lake, but Storm got there first. She hauled Axus out of the water, but a fearsome fish already had his leg in its clutches, and no matter how hard Storm pulled, it pulled harder.

Storm sent a bolt of magic into the creature, just as an enormous mouth rose up around them. The fish fell away, into the maw of the colossal beast, and Storm jerked back as the mouth broke the surface. Storm flew up as fast as she knew how, but still the monster caught

161

Axus' breeches, tearing off a chunk of fabric before sinking back into the dark.

'Dad!' shouted Regio. 'Are you okay?'

Axus grunted, blood dripping from his leg, but he spread his wings and lifted his weight from Storm's grasp, so Storm almost missed it when Pips dropped from Gabriel's arms. For a moment, her heart lurched, but then light glinted off the tether in his hand, and his feet planted on the back of a rising Scarani.

The serpent was so big, five people could have stood abreast on its scaled back, and when it lifted its head free of the water, six sets of fangs protruded from its strange, smiling mouth, three on the top, and three on the bottom.

Pips didn't hesitate before throwing his tether around the monster's thick neck, then yanked hard enough to make its smile turn into a snarl. But despite its fury, the Scarani began to swim, Pips keeping its head up with the tether, directing it back towards the shore.

Storm held her breath. She hadn't dared hope they would achieve their goal on the first run. She'd thought they would perhaps make the beasts surface, and maybe have a successful touch down. She had never dreamed Pips would successfully ride one this time.

But he was doing it, the monster cutting smoothly through the water, its enormous, serpentine body stretching out behind, too long to see.

They continued towards the shore, Storm's heart in her mouth, until they were so close, Storm started to believe it might actually be this easy. But as they neared, a vibration spread out across the surface a hundred paces from the slipway, and a wall of water began to rise. 'Shit,' said Storm, under her breath. 'Pips!' she shouted. 'Can you steer around?'

But it was futile, for the wall was widening, stretching out on each side, cutting them off from the sloped ground they needed to land the monster. And anyway, Pips was concentrating so hard he didn't seem to hear her.

'Shit.'

'Storm!' shouted Regio, his voice panicked.

Storm turned, and the sight greeting her nearly sent her plummeting into the lake. '*Warrior* ...'

Gabriel flew for his son, whose face was glowing gold, his scales alight and shining like a beacon.

The beast Pips rode bucked under his feet, fighting the tether, and Pips cast his eyes skyward, looking for Storm ... for his escape.

Gabriel plucked Veau from Regio's grasp, but the water below them was a roiling mass of white, every creature seeming to have been drawn to the surface.

'I must warn Isa,' said Axus. He darted forward, heading for the wall of water, which now entirely blocked their path, stretching to the ceiling and each wall. Axus plowed into the barrier, his hands held out before him like a diver. He made it only halfway through before some force stopped him dead.

'Dad!' Regio screamed for the third time. 'No!'

Storm flew for Pips, for the Children had made the barrier, and it would surely do the same to the beast Pips rode.

She reached him as the Scarani hit with a shuddering force so strong the wall bent before their eyes. Storm grabbed Pips before he was thrown forward into the wall, only narrowly avoiding the monster's body, which was lifting out of the water in a wave.

The wall sprang straight, and the Scarani's raised body slammed against it, causing a shockwave that threw them all backwards. They regained their balance, but the force cut Axus in half, his torso stuck in the wall, his legs falling into the water to be eaten by the creatures below.

'No!' Regio screamed, his wild, terrified eyes finding Storm.

'The tunnels,' shouted Gabriel, flying to the side, but an eerie silence descended, everything going still, the wall no longer rippling. Gabriel stopped, looking back at Storm with a question in his eyes.

A disturbance speared through the water below, and the hairs on Storm's arms stood on end. The wall of water fell, Axus' body disappearing under the lake, the Scarani floating for a moment before it too began to sink.

Storm held her breath, willing her mind to think, but then lights began circling under the water, and a lead weight dropped through her stomach.

She met Gabriel's eyes and screamed, 'Run!'

Chapter Twelve

THE ENTRANCE TO THE tunnel out of the mountain was so close, Storm could almost touch it. Regio flew ahead, saying something about the Black Guild and a woman called Ivka. Storm shouted to him, trying to make him come with them, to leave the mountain, but he disappeared down a side tunnel, and Storm let him go. If he wasn't willing to save himself, there was little she could do.

Storm weaved through the tunnels at breakneck speed, still carrying Pips, Gabriel following with Veau. They shouted to everyone they saw, telling them to leave the mountain, that the Children of the Lake were rising to retake their home.

Most didn't understand the threat. They sent frowns and skeptical looks, and some even laughed.

'Laugh all you want,' shouted Storm, 'but if you don't leave, you will die!' A few faltered at that, but she didn't wait to see if they heeded her warning.

They were almost to the southern entrance when Isa materialized before them. 'Stop,' she said, holding out her hand, her palm towards them.

They had little choice but to do as she said, for under the mountain, no one had the power to defy a direct order from their leader. Storm set Pips down, and Gabriel did the same to Veau, although he kept hold of his son's arm, not taking any chances.

'Isa,' said Gabriel, his voice placating, 'we must leave the mountain. All of us. The Children …'

'*She* has turned them against us,' said Isa, the words a snarl.

'No,' said Gabriel. 'I was there—and Pips and Veau—we saw it with our own eyes.'

'She planned it all; worked with them.'

'Isa,' said Gabriel, stepping towards her, finally releasing Veau, 'you know Storm didn't cause this, but at this moment, it matters not. All that matters is saving our people. You must evacuate the mountain.'

'Never,' said Isa. 'I will never …'

'Then you condemn them all to death,' said Storm, 'for the Children will suck them dry.'

'Storm,' said Gabriel, his tone sharp.

Storm closed her eyes and bunched her fists, but said no more.

'Isa,' said Gabriel, 'go to the long-lives in the depths, tell them what is happening. Save them.'

'Why would I help them?' said Isa. 'I have slaved to keep us safe, to make us prosperous in our jail, and what have they done? Sat beneath the mountain, reaping the benefits and doing nothing in return.'

Storm had to admit, Isa wasn't wrong, but that was what Isa had wanted in the beginning; to run the show with no interference. That it had worn her down was no surprise, but it was Isa's own doing.

A ruckus sounded behind them, and Storm's eyes darted back over her shoulder. 'They're coming,' she said. 'I can feel it.'

'Naturally,' said Isa, 'for your magic is their magic, is it not? You're nothing but a filthy *human*, and those wicked creatures made you the freak you are. Now they've come to take it away. Ironic, don't you think?'

'They come for us all,' said Storm, ignoring the wary looks Veau and Pips cast her way. 'They may take me, but make no mistake, you're high on their list.'

Isa moved with no warning. She disappeared, then reappeared behind Storm in less than a heartbeat. Isa wrapped an arm around Storm's neck, and it was all Storm could do to get her hands up to protect her windpipe.

'If you can no longer help with the Children, there is no longer a reason for me to keep you alive,' said Isa, squeezing ever harder.

'Worried I'll tell the world what you're really like?' Storm choked. 'That you're a liar and a cheat? That you think yourself superior ...'

'I am not ...'

'You lied about your son ... about Leo,' said Storm.

Isa's grip loosened enough that Storm could elbow her in the stomach. Isa fell back a pace, and Storm spun free, Isa's focus now on Gabriel.

'Don't look at him,' spat Storm. 'He hates you ... that you trapped him ... that you *forced* him.' She said the words through gritted teeth, wanting nothing more than to rip Isa's throat out, but while they were under the mountain, her hands were tied.

'You don't know what it is,' said Isa, 'to love like I do. You are not from my line ... have never experienced the mad rush of compulsion. The magic doesn't care who you love, but it chose Gabriel for me.

We serve a higher purpose, and you are nothing but a test for us both.'

'You don't speak for Gabriel or the magic,' said Storm.

'How dare you? You don't even have magic of your own!'

'Our father's blood runs in both of us,' said Storm. 'Even if that eats you up inside.'

'Wait,' said Veau, turning his still-glowing face to Gabriel. 'They're sisters?'

Gabriel inclined his head a fraction.

'You are a freak!' Isa screamed, suddenly close, nothing Storm could do to stop the punch to her gut. 'You are nothing!'

Storm doubled over and clutched her stomach. 'I am as much of something as anyone else,' she wheezed. 'We allowed you to lead because we pitied you, but we should never have done so.'

Storm could feel the Children destroying many they could save. It sent panic rippling through her blood, making her jittery. They had to find a way past Isa, and avoid her ordering them back into the mountain. And they had to do it quickly.

'*Allowed it?*' Isa sneered. 'Like you could have stopped me! Pure, high fae magic runs in my veins.'

'The high fae are a fiction. You're obsessed with placing yourself above others, of finding false reasons to demand respect and dominance. You and your mother both …'

'Do not speak of my mother when yours was a human whore!' Isa screamed.

'She was not, and our father loved her even though she had no magic. Maybe because your mother such a power-hungry bitch, while mine was gentle and kind.'

'Liar!'

'You're the liar. You hid Leo and Veau from your supposed true love.'

'He is my true love!'

'No, he is not. He doesn't love you, and the only reason you wanted him was because he wanted me. You couldn't bear that a big, powerful fae male would choose me over you.'

'He is high fae, and you are an abomination!' Isa punched Storm again, then whirled to face Gabriel. 'My love, you must understand, I hid Leo for the good of us all. For his own safety …'

'Is that why you hid Veau, too?' said Gabriel, his tone giving nothing away.

Isa took a step towards where Gabriel, Pips, and Veau stood, backed up against the wall. 'I did that for you … to spare you the pain of having such a son …'

They couldn't let Isa get too close, lest she snatch Veau and hold him hostage. Storm didn't know for sure if Gabriel would sacrifice himself for his son, but it was likely, and she could not let that happen.

'Did you try to kill Veau too?' said Storm. 'As you tried to kill me? Or was it always your plan to use him as leverage over Gabriel?'

Isa kept edging towards the group.

'I can only imagine what you put your own son through,' Storm continued, desperately searching for the right button to push. 'Although, with a mother like yours, I suppose you don't know any different. You're ignorant.'

Isa stopped but didn't turn around.

'And the ridiculous halting speech you use to make yourself seem special. You never did that when we were children …'

Isa was behind Storm in a blink, this time raining punches everywhere her fists could reach. Storm ducked and turned, but Isa followed, knocking her to the floor, sitting on her stomach.

'I should have killed you when we were children,' Isa hissed, throwing punch after terrible punch, 'before you tricked the Children into sharing their evil powers.'

Storm surged upwards, flying for the ceiling. She did not intend to harm Isa, and therefore the magic did not restrict her; Isa was merely in the way, her back striking the rock a tick before she magicked herself free. When she reappeared, it was in a heap on the ground, her eyes suddenly misty.

Neither Gabriel nor Storm missed a beat. They grabbed the others and launched themselves further along the tunnels, until finally they passed under the strange portcullis made of cogs and vials that marked the entrance to the mountain. It was open—thank all the Gods—nor did it come crashing down atop them.

A gaggle of Fae'ch had already gathered outside, and Storm shouted for them to move back, to flee down the mountain. The Children would pick off those inside first, but once they'd finished there, they might come outside.

Isa screamed behind them, perched on the mountain's threshold, refusing to give up even with her power over them lost. 'Gabriel! My love! Come back to me,' she pleaded, holding out her hands.

'Save your people,' said Gabriel. 'You're the only one who can.'

'Axus should have closed the portcullis,' said Isa, seeming suddenly confused. 'He has never failed me before.'

'Axus is dead,' said Gabriel, taking a small step towards her.

'Yes,' said Isa, 'come to me.' Her eyes gleamed, and Gabriel stopped dead.

'Tell the long-lives,' said Gabriel. 'They must help you transport our people out of the mountain. We need them. We need powerful magics if we are to survive this ... whatever this is.'

Isa cocked her head to one side. 'Will you come with me?' she said, her voice a childish simper.

Rage boiled in Storm's chest.

'I cannot,' said Gabriel. 'I do not have that form of magic.' He spoke slowly, as though explaining something to an infant. 'But you must go now, and I will see you when you return. Be quick, for we do not know how far the Children have already travelled. Show me—show us all—how mighty you are.'

Bile rose in Storm's throat as she watched Gabriel manage Isa. She wondered if this was what it had always been like between them, at least when Isa wasn't making him bed other women, or forcing herself upon him ...

Isa thought for a moment and then nodded. She disappeared, and Storm was tempted to flee, but Gabriel stayed rooted to the spot.

A group of long-lives appeared, including Michael, and many of the others who had assisted Gabriel in Fairy Land.

'Gods,' said Michael, shaking his head. 'I never thought I'd see you out of the mountain again, old friend.'

Isa reappeared moments later, tugging a stubborn child behind her. She pushed the child into the crowd, then looked to Gabriel for praise.

Storm clenched her teeth as Gabriel sent her encouraging, admiring words.

Isa disappeared again, and another large group of long-lives appeared around them. 'Thank you,' a fae woman said to an ancient-looking man.

He nodded, then disappeared, presumably heading back for more.

Storm ushered everyone away from the entrance. She sent them along a mighty canyon lined with metal cogs towards the path that led down the mountain, into the Kingdom of Starlight. They needed space for anyone else they could rescue, and she wanted a clear path to safety as soon as they could leave.

Minutes ticked by, and then screams and cries echoed out of the mountain, the sounds of brutal deaths and prolonged suffering. Isa returned with a bleeding hand, her hair disheveled, and collapsed to the ground.

'It is over,' said Isa, her voice little more than a whisper. She waved a hand, and the portcullis whirled shut. 'Those inside are lost.'

Storm cast around for Regio's tall, broad form, but couldn't find him. Her chest tightened and her breaths became shallow. Somewhere along the way she'd come to like the cocky lordling, and a pang of loss hit her hard in the chest.

'Move!' Storm shouted to everyone present, holding out her hand to Gabriel. 'We must leave now, before the Children follow.'

'You must return inside the mountain,' said Isa, struggling to her feet, her face twisted into a cruel smile.

Storm gave her an incredulous look. 'That would be suicide.'

'You are the only one who can placate the Children,' said Isa. 'That is the one benefit you bring our kind … why we tolerate your theatrics.' Isa's eyes flashed dangerously, the threat in them crystal clear. It was one thing to reveal Storm's secret to Veau and Pips, but quite another to announce it to the enormous group of assembled long-lives.

'There is no placating the Children,' said Gabriel, stepping up beside Storm. 'They're in a feeding frenzy … ripping the mountain apart.'

Isa's eyes went wide and furious, presumably because Gabriel had sided with Storm, undermining Isa in such a public way. 'She is one of them,' said Isa, pointing an accusatory finger at Storm. 'She belongs with them, not with us.'

Many around them gasped, and some even moved back.

'Incorrect,' said Storm, stepping towards Isa. For the first time in hundreds of years, Storm no longer had to keep herself in check. They were outside the mountain, free of the binding oath to obey. Isa was no longer their leader, for her domain spread to the edge of the mountain and no further. And Gabriel was outside too, and Veau. Isa had run out of leverage, and the realization sent a thrill down Storm's spine.

'You are an abomination!' spat Isa.

'No more so than you,' said Storm, a smile on her lips, 'for you have let our skills perish. Perhaps you even engineered it that way. You have always been quite fond of the notion that fae are superior to the rest of our kind … something you learned from your witch of a mother.'

'You do not deserve to breathe the same air as the magic-born.'

'You're just pissed our father liked me better, as does Gabriel.'

'The Children gave you your magic!' screamed Isa, for that was the only leverage that remained. All she had left.

'They did,' said Storm, 'because when others plotted ways to kill them, I treated them kindly and with respect. Had I not done so, you think we would have found refuge these past few hundred years?'

'I will kill you for this slaughter,' Isa screeched. She stepped forward menacingly, her hands outstretched.

'The Fae'ch protects anyone with magic,' said Michael, his tone light but firm. He stepped out of the crowd, standing shoulder to shoulder with Storm and Gabriel. 'That was what we agreed in the beginning, when we fled to the mountain.'

Isa turned wrathful eyes on Michael. 'You are outlawed,' she said, through gritted teeth.

'In case you hadn't noticed,' Michael said with a laugh, 'we are all outlawed … and not for the first time.'

'And if we don't get moving, we will all be without our lives,' said Storm.

'If you leave now, you may never return,' said Isa, her desperate eyes locked on Gabriel.

Storm let Isa see the pity she felt. 'You no longer control us,' she said. 'The Children have reclaimed their domain, and with it, your position as our leader.'

'We are homeless,' said Gabriel.

'Not quite,' said Storm, shaking her head, 'for Queen Fyia has promised us a place in her lands.' Storm turned to Veau, who had the look of a rabbit caught in torchlight. Storm cocked an expectant eyebrow.

'Yes,' said Veau, hesitantly, then more firmly, 'Yes. My sister has magic of her own. She is a friend to the Fae'ch. She wants to work with us …'

'Us?' said Isa. 'You are not one of us.'

'The Fae'ch protects anyone with magic,' Michael repeated, 'and Veau has more than many born under the mountain.'

'You've seen to that, sister,' said Storm.

Isa ignored the snipe, her eyes flicking from Michael to Gabriel.

'We have no choice,' said Gabriel. 'To stay here is to die.'

'Gabriel,' said Isa, 'my love. Come with me.'

Gabriel's features were a carefully schooled mask, so even Storm couldn't read his emotions. Her heart jumped into her throat as she waited for his response. She knew, logically, Gabriel would choose her over any other, but still ...

Isa's face screwed into an agitated ball. 'I have tolerated your bit on the side for long enough,' she said, trying to sound commanding, 'but she's imp-cap crazy. She cannot join us.'

Gabriel took Storm's hand. 'I won't argue with you, Isa, she may well be imp-cap crazy. But I love her. I do not love you ... never have. You abused your position and our trust, abused me in abominable ways, punished Storm for the actions of your father ...'

Gabriel looked lovingly down at Storm, and she smiled warmly back at him. 'We will go to the Queen of the Five Kingdoms,' he said, raising his voice so all could hear, 'for there is a disturbance in the air, and Queen Fyia will need those with magic to help her. She believes in a better, fairer future, and I for one applaud her.'

'You are welcome to join us,' said Storm, squeezing Gabriel's hand. 'To make a new life for yourselves in the light.'

And then she started walking, Gabriel by her side, Veau and Pips only a pace behind. Michael's winged form passed overhead, and Storm could feel the others filing after them, but she didn't look back. At last it was over ... the mountain, Isa, sharing Gabriel, life in the darkness. It had been hundreds of years, but finally, finally, they could go home.

I hope you enjoyed House of Storms and Secrets, and if you did, would really appreciate a review wherever you buy books or on social media. If you don't have time to write a review, just a star rating is very much appreciated, and makes a huge difference to authors in this algorithm driven world ...

Want more from the *Shadow and Ash* world? To read Alba and Leo's story, sign up to my newsletter here: https://www.subscribepage.com/r2a0n6_copy and get *The Water Rider and the High Born Fae* for free (or you can buy it for 99c if you're not a newsletter person!). And if you want to know more about Queen Fyia, read on for a preview of *Kingdoms of Shadow and Ash*.

PREVIEW OF KINGDOMS OF SHADOW
AND ASH

Chapter One

FYIA CREPT AROUND THE circular battlement, her heart thundering in her chest, her back pressed against the cold, hard stone. The big, full moon cast eerie shadows, and every flicker sent adrenaline through her veins.

King Perdes lay in wait, but he didn't know from which side she would approach, and Fyia wanted to keep it that way.

I am not a warrior. I am not a warrior. I am not a warrior. She silently chanted the words like a prayer; a reminder she had to be smart. She was swift, and she was nimble, and she was stealthy.

She inched further around the battlement, looking down at her black pants and tunic one last time, making sure nothing would reflect the moonbeams. She'd smeared her face and hands with mud, her hat pulled low on her brow, hiding the shock of white that punctuated her long brown hair.

I am not a warrior.

She took one torturous sidestep at a time, placing each foot with extreme care. Three steps and she would be in sight.

Fyia summoned her power, a wild pull of magic, and called to her Cruaxee. An eagle—her eagle—cried out in the distance. Perdes inhaled sharply and shuffled his feet. She let silence fall until it yawned menacingly into the night.

'No. Stay back,' said Perdes, his voice directed to the other side of the battlements. No surprise, given the two wolves she'd sent to stare him down.

I am not a warrior. But …

She ran on light feet, making no sound, then leapt, her wolves snarling, keeping Perdes engaged. She sank her dagger into his back once, twice, then pulled it out, whirling away as he tried to face her. He looked surprised as he collapsed to the floor.

'Filthy cheat,' he spluttered, wheezing through the blood.

Fyia leaned against the battlements, her wolves coming to her side. She wiped and sheathed her dagger. 'Well, here's the thing, Perdes … I wouldn't have won if I'd challenged you to a fair fight.'

'Women have no honor.'

'You want those to be your last words?'

'My army will defeat you.'

'Last I checked, your commanders had surrendered, and were drinking with my generals in my war tent.'

'My people will never follow you,' he choked, blood leaking from his mouth. 'They follow warriors, kings, not *little women.*'

Fyia laughed. 'You're right, I'm no warrior. I am not tall and broad and formidable to look at. But turns

179

out I can stick a dagger in a man's back just fine. Not to mention, I have a few assets you do not …'

'*Witch* …' He made a disgusting gurgling noise, and then his eyes fluttered closed.

'Careful, if the Fae'ch hear you, they'll curse your afterlife … they would never class *me* among their ranks.'

'You are nothing next to me …' He dragged in a breath. 'I am a king!'

'And yet, I have my army, yours too, my magic, and, oh yes, I have a brain—something you lack … something all of you lacked. You got fat and lazy, and I conquered five kingdoms. I believe I'm the only leader alive who can lay claim to that.'

He grunted, but no words followed.

Fyia crouched by his side and watched as he took his last labored breath, then reached down and removed his crown. She'd put it with the others … she'd cast it into the fiery pits of Hell.

Fyia walked out under the portcullis, then across the bridge over the castle's moat, her wolves flanking her. She'd removed her hat, and her hair flowed freely down her back, Perdes' crown perched atop her head.

Her generals waited, a sea of lower-ranking commanders behind them. She emerged like an angel of death, a witch, someone to be feared, her beasts snarling at her side.

Sensis Deimos, the leader of Fyia's victorious army, stepped forward, throwing herself to her knees before her Queen. The others did the same, no one daring to look up. They barely dared to breathe.

'Rise, Sensis,' said Fyia. Sensis was tall and powerfully built, with long, plaited auburn hair and pale green eyes. 'Do something with this, until we can rid ourselves of the gaudy thing.' She threw Perdes' crown, and Sensis caught it with ease.

'Of course, Your Majesty,' said Sensis, bowing her head.

Fyia offered Sensis her forearm, and her general clasped it, her grip brutal. Fyia pulled Sensis in until their bodies collided, Fyia's head reaching just above her friend's shoulder, and Sensis slapped her on the back.

'You can get a five-pointed crown now,' Sensis said, her voice pitched low so none of the others could hear. 'Maybe with a gem from each kingdom ... it would set off your pretty blue witch eyes.'

'Piss off,' said Fyia. 'Actually, don't ... do something useful and get a celebration going.'

'It is my greatest honor to serve you in any way you desire,' she said. She stepped back and bowed low.

'Don't make me punch you in the face.'

'If you're going to threaten violence, at least make it realistic.' Fyia's wolves growled. 'See, now I'm scared.'

'Good. I'm ...' Fyia trailed off, her gaze finding the woods beyond her general's shoulder.

'Go,' said Sensis. 'I'll hold down the fort until you return.' Sensis surveyed the curious commanders. They were still on their knees, most chancing glances at their Queen. 'King Perdes is dead,' she said, in a voice that carried ... a voice used to being obeyed. 'Long live Fyia Orlightus, Queen of the Five Kingdoms of the East.'

Fyia acknowledged the cheers of her army, a thrill travelling up her spine at what she'd accomplished. What they'd all accomplished.

Fyia took off into the woods, her army still chanting her name, Sensis issuing orders, quieting them down.

Fyia's shoeless feet ate up the ground, each pace renewing her connection with the forest. She drew on the power it offered, letting it fill her, pushing out the terror that lingered from the battlements. Her wolves chased her, pushing her faster, others joining them, snarling as they ran. Fyia pumped her arms, sprinting, flying, letting the forest show her the way.

She broke through the tree line, heading for the sheer drop over a cliff not fifty paces away. The wolves fell back, snarling as she ran for the edge, their discomfort peppering the bond between them. Fyia didn't falter, didn't miss a step as she threw herself into the void, her arms outstretched.

The wolves howled, and Fyia gasped, relishing the rush of wind that bit her skin.

She fell and fell and laughed, knowing it would kill her. At this speed, if she hit the river, the impact would be fatal, but the rush … the rush chased all the things she needed it to away. It left freedom … euphoria.

An eagle screamed below, and Fyia closed her eyes, connecting with her Cruaxee, watching through the eagle's eyes as the enormous bird swooped under her, caught her, slowed her fall, then reversed it.

The pump of the eagle's wings made Fyia's stomach drop, and she laughed again. They climbed, and she shivered with anticipation, excitement flooding her when she felt the downward tip, the beginning of a dive. Only when they were hurtling towards the ground once more did it finally begin to sink in: she was Queen of the Five Kingdoms.

She'd done it; what everyone had said she could never do ... that she *should* not do ... that the magic would not tolerate. They'd been wrong; the magic had wanted her to win, had aided her at every turn. Of course it had. She had a Cruaxee, was magic-touched, and fire-touched— even if only a little. She had more magic than most could ever dream of.

And finally, it was done ... she'd slain the old Kings and united five kingdoms. She ruled them all.

Adigos stalked through the camp, past fire after fire, group after group of drunken soldiers. They didn't care who'd won the war, not really. They only cared it was over, that they could go back to their children, wives, and lovers. They drank, not because Fyia had united their five bickering kingdoms, but because they hoped to never dig latrines again. To never march day and night to outsmart their enemy. To never face another battlefield, nor lose friends to an enemy blade. They rejoiced, for they would eat slops no more—at least if their purses could afford it.

They were drunk and spirited, and it was contagious.

Adigos walked and walked, careful to keep to the shadows. He passed brawls, card games, bodies passed out on the floor, bodies writhing against each other, all manner of sounds escaping into the night. He was jealous of their carefree existence, if only for this one night. He'd had that once, and he wanted it again.

He finally reached the barn near the castle's walls. The invading forces had commandeered it for their officers' mess, and the sounds of a party blared from inside. But outside, the mood was tense.

The Queen's bodyguard stood watch, guarding a twenty-pace perimeter around the building, and those at the campfires were subdued, brooding, the air heavy with some unspoken threat.

Adigos paused at a fire close to the perimeter where an old man warmed himself. The man watched the barn intently, not seeming to notice Adigos.

'May I sit?' Adigos asked.

The man's head turned, his features cast in shadow. 'If you must.'

'Not celebrating?' said Adigos, lowering himself onto a tree stump. This far south, it was warm most of the year, but the nights were cool, and Adigos held out his hands to the fire, the familiar habit comforting.

'What is there to celebrate? My King is dead, and now we have a *witch* queen.' He practically spat the words.

'You liked King Perdes?' asked Adigos, picking up a stick and poking at the embers.

'Served him my whole life.'

'Was he a good king?'

'Was to me.'

'To his people? Did they love him?'

'You're not from these lands?' said the man. He scrutinized Adigos anew.

'No,' said Adigos, 'and I've been away awhile. Did they? Love him? They loved the King in my lands before she ...'

The man nodded his wizened features, as though Adigos had just fallen into place in his mind. 'I can't say they all did, but I did, and I'm not alone.' His words were menacing and full of promise. Not everyone would make things easy on the new Queen, then.

The man turned back to the barn, and Adigos followed his gaze. A flicker of movement in the trees caught Adigos' attention. He watched carefully as a shadow crept from trunk to trunk, and a slow, victorious smile spread across his lips.

'Have a good evening,' said Adigos, getting to his feet. The man made a non-committal noise, and Adigos melted into the woods, trailing the shadow he'd come to see.

Adigos crept through the woods, staying downwind, placing his feet with the utmost care, so as not to snap a twig or stumble on a root. The moon shone brightly, the trees sparse, allowing him to see a way ahead, and he finally spotted her, leaning against a tree. She observed the back entrance to the barn, and his pulse quickened. She was out here all alone, and she hadn't sensed him …

Adigos unsheathed his dagger and moved forward, praying she would stay put, that she was too preoccupied to feel his approach. He used the cover of the shadows, the sounds of the hooting owls and rattle of the snakes, the wind creaking the branches and rustling the leaves.

She shifted, pushing away from the tree as though finally deciding to go inside, but Adigos was so close he could almost touch her, and he would not let her get away. He lunged, grabbing her waist with one hand, holding his dagger to her throat with the other, relishing the power he held in his hands.

'It's not safe out in the woods alone,' Adigos growled into her ear.

'I'm never alone …' The woman tipped back her head and walked her fingers up his arm. She found his head, which still hovered near her ear, and grabbed a handful of his hair. She tugged, just hard enough to make him part his lips. She did it again, and he had to fight the urge to groan. 'Took you long enough,' said his Queen.

He ran his nose down her neck. 'You knew I was here?'

'My wolves picked up your scent days ago. Why did you wait so long?'

'After what happened last time, I thought it better to … gather intelligence.'

'Wise choice.'

Adigos brushed his lips against her neck. She shivered, then pushed his dagger arm away. She faced him, his arm still on her waist, and he pulled her towards him, lowering his head.

She shoved him away. 'Debrief me after the feast.'

He could do nothing but watch as she made her way towards the barn, two of her wolves appearing out of the darkness to walk at her side. Adigos took a deep breath, clearing his lungs of her intoxicating scent, then trailed in her wake.

The barn—which Sensis had done a passable job of turning into a feasting hall—went silent when Fyia entered. All except Rouel—a member of her personal guard who could have made a lucrative living as a minstrel—who was in the middle of a particularly catchy refrain. He sketched a bow that had his hand skimming the floor, staying down until he finished the song. Fyia shot him an arch look as she walked to the makeshift dais and throne.

She sat, and her wolves lay at her feet. 'Continue,' she said, gesturing to Rouel to get on with it. Music flared from his lute, and the party resumed. She ignored the incessant looks in her direction, most furtive, but plenty blatant.

Sensis, and Edu Ceres, the head of her personal guard, approached the dais. They made a show of bowing low before Fyia beckoned them forward, so they could take their places behind her, one on each side. They looked remarkably similar to one another, the same height, broad shoulders, straight noses, and fair skin, although Edu's muscles seemed somehow less impressive, and he had a shock of white hair, tied back in a bun.

'Fun party,' said Fyia, sardonically. She hated these things, but knew them to be a necessary evil. It was better for her subjects to see who she really was than create a persona of their own, and she enjoyed watching her wolves fan the flames of the fear her reputation had already kindled. 'Anyone I should worry about?'

'No,' said Sensis, at the same time as Edu said, 'Yes.'

Sensis rolled her eyes. 'You take things too seriously, my friend.'

'That's my job,' said Edu. 'I have one person to keep alive. If you lose a few on the battlefield, that's war. If I lose Fyia ...'

'It's called taking calculated risks to ensure victory, and we're here, so I'd say it paid off,' said Sensis. 'It's no different with the safety of our Queen ... maybe you should try it sometime and let her enjoy herself.'

'The day I start taking notes from you is the day we should cast our eyes to the line of succession ...'

'There's a line of succession?' said Sensis.

Fyia could hear the smile on Sensis' lips, and was sure Edu would be fighting one of his own. There was no line of succession—as her critics kept reminding her—but that was a problem for another day.

'Are you two done?' said Fyia.

187

'For now,' said Sensis.

'What concerns you, Edu?'

'The big one over there,' said Edu.

Fyia found the very large, very attractive man gesticulating in their general direction.

'Who is he?' said Fyia.

Sensis laughed. 'He's King Perdes' distant cousin. The rest of his family fled when they realized they'd lost.'

'He's taking a ... different approach,' said Edu.

'Which is?' asked Fyia.

'You'll see,' said Sensis, doing a poor job of hiding her amusement.

'Oh, Mother ...' said Fyia. She fought to keep her expression neutral as the man began moving towards the dais.

'Don't pray to her,' said Sensis. 'She can't help you.'

'Then who would you suggest?'

'The Warrior,' said Edu, 'to help you fight him off.'

'The Whore,' said Sensis. 'Might give you some tips.'

'Helpful,' said Fyia.

'The Friend,' said Rouel, who had perched his slight frame on the edge of the dais, 'to tell you nothing about that man looks problematic at all.'

'Or ... oh, my ...' said Sensis. 'Maybe you should seek help from a jealous almost-former-lover ...'

Adigos had just slipped in through the door.

'Wait, they never did it?' said Edu, looking to Sensis for confirmation.

'I don't think they ever did ... wait, did you?' said Sensis.

'Could we deal with one problem at a time?' said Fyia. She eyed Perdes' cousin, who was getting dangerously close, and seemed a little unsteady on his feet.

'Is Adigos still a problem?' said Sensis. 'Have you been holding out on me?'

'I feel a song coming on ...' said Rouel.

One of Fyia's wolves growled, and they all fell silent. The growling, they had learned the hard way, wasn't just for show.

'My Queen,' said Perdes' cousin, bowing low.

'Yes?' she said, fixing her face into a bored mask.

He looked up from his bow, unsure of what to do. 'May I ... approach?'

'No,' said Fyia.

'May I ... um ... stand?'

'If you must.'

He hesitated for a moment before raising himself to his full height. 'Your Majesty, I am Lord Max Perdes, cousin of the former King Perdes. May I be the first to declare fealty to you, and to request your hand in marriage?'

Fyia cocked a mocking eyebrow, but he continued, seeming not to have noticed. 'I have extensive lands, lucrative trading connections in the west, and ...' he leaned in conspiratorially, '... I'm working on a trade agreement with the kingdom in the north ... with the Black Hoods.'

It was all Fyia could do not to laugh out loud. The Black Hoods traded with nobody, save for the Fae'ch, who were just as secretive.

'I appreciate your offer, my lord, and am glad of your fealty, but I decline the proposal of marriage. Enjoy the celebration.'

He furrowed his brow then took a step forward, apparently not used to rejection. His good looks and connections meant he'd probably never heard the word *no*, his life no-doubt full of fawning sycophants.

Everything in the room went still, all eyes on the man approaching their Queen without leave. Edu and

Sensis stepped forward, but Fyia sent them an almost imperceptible head shake; she wanted to see what this fool would do. He stopped in front of the wolves, who had lifted their heads, yellow eyes fixed on the threat.

'That's it?' he said. 'You won't even let me court you? Our match would be advantageous to all five of your kingdoms ...'

Fyia looked at him, but said not a word, her face giving nothing away.

He frowned, waiting for her to say something, then fidgeted, his gaze flitting as uncertainty crept in.

Fyia tilted her head to the side and watched him closely. He bowed, finally realizing his mistake, and Fyia waved her hand, shooing him away. He went without protest, and the room breathed a collective sigh of relief.

By the time the party died down, Fyia had received three marriage proposals. The one from Max Perdes, of the Sky Kingdom, one from a merchant from the Kingdom of the Moon, and one from a former Princess of the Kingdom of Sea Serpents. Nobody from her homeland—the Starlight Kingdom—would be so stupid as to propose marriage, leaving only the Kingdom of Plenty unrepresented. Maybe they were more sensible, or less drunk, or maybe they'd lost courage after the first three rejections. Either way, she was happy when the night drew to a close.

'Kick them out,' Fyia said to Edu when she could take no more. Edu summoned Fyia's personal guard, who saw to it that every last person found the door, leaving only Edu, Sensis, and Adigos, who'd been skulking at the back all night.

'Adi!' said Sensis, approaching Adigos with her arms wide open. She embraced him. 'Long time.'

'I went as fast as I could.' His eyes flicked to Fyia as she lowered herself beside the fire pit.

'Gods, it feels good to lie down,' she said. She rolled onto her back, one of her wolves nuzzling her arm.

'It feels good the war is over,' said Sensis.

'Don't get too comfortable,' said Fyia. 'We're leaving tomorrow.'

'We are?' said Sensis.

'Well, not you. You'll need to stay, and … you know … lead the army, but the rest of us.'

'Where are we going?' said Edu.

'To the ford town in Plenty—Selise. I intend to build a new palace there.'

'Why there?' asked Adigos.

'It's a central spot between all five kingdoms … or at least as central as it's possible to be. It's prosperous, easy to access, and good for trade. I've sent Essa an eagle; she'll meet us there.'

'To design the palace?' said Sensis.

Fyia nodded. 'She won't be happy I'm dragging her away from her workshop, but she's the only one I trust.'

The following morning, Fyia, Edu, and Adigos mounted their horses. Fyia was restless and couldn't wait to get going. She had few friends in the Sky Kingdom—something she would have to rectify.

Eagles circled overhead, screaming as they swooped, chafing against the Cruaxee bond.

'They want to go home?' asked Adigos, manoeuvring his skittish mare next to Fyia's stallion.

'Their work is done, and they long to be free.' She closed her eyes, reaching for the magic binding them to her. She tugged on the strings, then let them go, feeling the eagles slide from her control. She opened her eyes as they cried out in farewell, flying north, back to the mountains they called home.

'We wouldn't have won without them,' said Edu, shielding his eyes against the rising sun.

'We owe them a great debt,' agreed Fyia. She shook off the sadness that washed over her. Her eagles urged her to go with them; they would miss her, as she would miss them. If only she could …

Two of her wolves stepped out of the woods, sensing her agitation.

'Will you let them go too?' asked Adigos.

'I've released the whole pack,' said Fyia. 'These two want to stay.' She urged her mount to a walk, heading for the trees.

'Surely you'll name them now?' said Adigos, falling in beside her.

'They're wild animals, not pets,' said Fyia.

'Well, if you won't, I will.'

Fyia rolled her eyes.

'The bigger one, let's call her …'

'Fluffy,' said Edu, smirking at Fyia's pained expression. 'What? She's very fluffy.'

'Keep up,' said Fyia, squeezing her legs. Her horse leapt into the air, and Fyia felt every excited bunch of his muscles, no saddle beneath her. He jumped again, then took off at a gallop, hurtling through the trees. Her wolves yipped with glee, racing alongside, Fyia's hair and cloak streaming out behind her.

Adigos' mare was fast, and he caught Fyia, whooping with excitement as he came level, narrowly avoiding a branch. They ran for another league before reining in their horses, walking to let Fyia's guard catch up.

'Gods, it's good to have some fun,' said Fyia.

'That it is,' said Adigos.

A twig snapped close to their left, and Adigos screamed, 'Down!' as an arrow passed a whisper from his ear.

'*Warrior*,' said Fyia, whirling back the way they'd come.

Adigos tried to follow, but his mount reared and bucked, an arrow buried in her rump. Adigos cried out, and Fyia reigned in her stallion as he was thrown from the saddle. He landed hard, letting out a grunt, his horse racing away.

Fyia was at Adigos' side in three ticks, but men and women approached from all directions. Her wolves snarled, then attacked, the sound of ripping flesh filling Fyia's ears as she tried to make sense of it all.

'Go!' cried Adigos. He winced as he rolled to his feet, drawing his sword. 'Run! I'll hold them off.'

But before she could, she fell, registering an impact against her shoulder. She hit the ground and it hurt everywhere. Her horse—not a part of her Cruaxee—fled, and then she was being yanked to her feet, pulled up by Adigos.

'Do you have a weapon?' he hissed, as the ring of armed men and women moved in.

Fyia counted twelve. Twelve—armed to the hilt—against two and her wolves. Fyia drew her dagger. 'This is all I have,' she said in a low voice.

'*By the Whore*,' said Adigos, assessing the threat. Fyia watched as his mind worked out their odds, calculating, then realizing their chances weren't good.

Silence settled as their attackers moved forward on soundless feet, step by step, never taking their eyes from Fyia.

A grunt of pain broke the silence, then a thud, the unexpected sounds distracting them all. Adigos and her wolves didn't miss a beat, lunging forward, taking the fight to their attackers.

I am not a warrior ...

'Behind that tree!' shouted Adigos, skewering the woman charging him.

Fyia moved, but was yanked back by her hair. She staggered back a pace, then whirled, surprising her attacker by grabbing his arm. He loosened his grip, and she spun herself around ... *but I can stab a man in the back just fine.*

The man went down just as a weight hit Fyia between the shoulders, throwing her forward, pinning her in place. Fists showered punch after punch on Fyia's head, neck, back. Fyia went limp, and the onslaught ceased. Her attacker's weight shifted forward, and Fyia grabbed her, rolling them over. She didn't hesitate for a tick before snatching up her dagger and sticking it in the woman's flesh. A woman who could not have been much older than Fyia's twenty-eight years.

The remaining attackers ran—only two still alive—and Fyia blinked as she took in the scene. Her bodyguards stood over the fallen, checking to make sure they were dead, blood and gore everywhere, littering the forest floor.

Edu and Adigos rushed to Fyia, dropping to their knees on either side of where she knelt. 'Are you hurt?' asked Adigos, his hands and eyes searching her for damage.

'I ...'

'There's blood coming from your shoulder. Get the healer!' Edu shouted at a guard.

'I can't see any other blood,' said Adigos.

'I'm fine,' said Fyia, pushing them off. 'Help me up.'

A horse with a fearsome woman atop screeched to a halt nearby. Sensis. She barked orders about perimeters, scouts, and only the Gods knew what else.

Fyia shot a look at Edu. 'We're in trouble now,' she said.

'What happened?' demanded Sensis. She slid off her horse and threw her reins to a soldier.

'We were attacked,' said Fyia.

Adigos rolled one of the dead onto his back. 'I spoke to this one last night,' he said. 'He told me Perdes was good to him.'

'Let's hope that's all this is,' said Sensis. 'We need to move, and I'm coming with you.'

Fyia's head went fuzzy, and she retched.

'*Mother* ...' said Adigos.

'Where's the healer?' Edu snapped.

'Get a carriage,' Sensis barked.

Fyia sank to the ground and let them fuss; it made little sense to argue when they were right.

Chapter Two

FYIA WOKE TO FIND herself in a plush carriage, her head in Adigos' lap, his hand stroking her hair. She tried to sit, but a blinding pain gripped her brain, so she gave up.

'What happened?' she asked, swotting away his hand. 'Is my horse okay?'

'The healer gave you something to knock you out. He said he told you to rest, and that you were being difficult. Your horse is fine. Mine is too, thank the Gods.'

'And? Do I have any lasting injuries?'

'You took an arrow to the shoulder, but it was only a flesh wound. The healer's more worried about pressure in your head, given the pounding it took. He instructed us to monitor you closely.'

'I'm fine. Help me up.'

Adigos slipped his hands under her and eased her up next to him. Her head pounded like it was under attack from ten thousand nails, but she forced herself to ignore the agony.

'Here,' said Adigos. He handed her a bundle of herbs. 'The healer said to chew these; it'll help with the pain.'

Fyia took them and looked out of the window as she bit down on the bitter green leaves. She could feel her wolves, glad they were safe, but scowled when she saw an entire squadron of soldiers escorting them. 'So much for travelling in secrecy,' she said.

'Sensis took over … you know how she is.'

She did know. Sensis was the best general the world had ever seen. She was ruthless, made hard decisions with empathy and conviction, never took chances she didn't have to, and inspired awe in those under her command, in everyone, really. Without Sensis, Fyia wouldn't be Queen of more than a single kingdom.

'Fyia, I'm …'

'Debrief me,' she said, cutting him off. Fyia wasn't in the mood to discuss how he'd betrayed her.

'I just …'

'Debrief me or leave. I have no wish to hear more of your apologies.'

He looked into her eyes, and she found a softness there she hadn't seen before. 'I missed you, and I'm glad to be back by your side.'

'It might not be for long if you make me ask a third time.'

Adigos held Fyia's gaze for a beat, then looked down at his hands. 'It's not what you want to hear.'

Fyia frowned. 'Did you even make it to the Fae'ch?'

'Please … give me some credit. I made it, they let me in, they even threw a party in my honor.'

'Insufferable hedonists.'

'That they are,' said Adigos, flashing a roguish smile.

'I don't need details of your debauchery.'

'Why?'

Her features set like stone. 'What did they say?'

'They said, if you want to know about their dragon egg, you should ask them yourself.'

'Did you snoop around?'

'I didn't get a chance. They watched me every tick I was there, which was all of a day before they kicked me out.'

'That's it?'

'I didn't see your brother, if that's what you mean.'

'Did you ask for him?'

'Should I have?'

'He was your best friend ...'

'He abandoned you.'

Fyia turned her gaze out of the window once more. 'He did what he needed to do.'

'You forgive him?'

'There's nothing to forgive.'

'Do you forgive me?' His words were a plea.

She closed her eyes, refusing to look at him. 'What you did will cast doubt on my legitimacy forever. It will add fuel to the arguments of my enemies ...'

'Fyia, I ...'

'You're sorry ... you regret it. You've said all the things you're supposed to say. But you defied a direct order. You made a kill that should have been mine.'

'You said yourself, you're not a warrior ...'

Fyia saw red, turning so fast she had to brace herself against the pain in her head. 'I'm Queen; I've never shied away from any part of that, including killing the men in my way.'

'I was trying to help.'

'You were trying to make a name for yourself ... to prove yourself the great warrior you think you are. You wanted glory, songs, women to fall at your feet ...' Even though they did that already. 'When I need help, I ask for it. You betrayed me, and I would've been within my rights to execute you.'

'But you didn't, because you knew sending me away would hurt me more. And it did hurt, every moment.'

'Because you longed to be in the middle of the action ... to be a part of the stories.'

'Because I longed to be with you.'

The blood drained from her brain as she looked into his eyes, flicking from one to the other, trying to see into his soul. He seemed to believe his words, but did he mean them? Would he make the right choice next time, or was his ego too strong to overrule ...?

Her head hurt.

'I've learned my lesson,' he said quietly. 'I will never disobey you again.'

'I can never trust you again ...' She wobbled, and had to grab his leg so as not to fall to the floor, the edges of her vision going black.

He took hold of her shoulders. 'You can,' he said, 'and I'll prove it, but right now you have to rest. You can't go into the Vipers' Nest like this.'

He was right, and better to sleep on Adigos than risk falling on the floor at every lurch of the carriage. She lifted her legs onto the cushioned red velvet bench, then rested her head in the crook of his shoulder. He dropped a muscular arm around her, and she nestled in, wrapping both of her arms around his much larger one. They'd travelled like this on countless occasions, and the familiarity was comforting. He was warm, and strong, and smelt faintly of leather, and not two turns of the carriage wheels later, she was asleep.

Fyia's carriage pulled up outside a colossal stone building. Copper runners zigzagged across the front, from the top, where a dragon clock ticked, all the way to the bottom, where the runners dipped into the small channel of water that circled the building.

Few dragon clocks existed, and the ones that did were spread across Fyia's kingdoms. The mechanisms were much like any other, but the numbers—one to twelve—started and finished either side of a dragon head, which sat where the number twelve would in any other clock.

They had once been used for more than just telling the time, or so said the legends, but for what, no one knew, at least in Fyia's five kingdoms. Magic had long been outlawed, and the fae and witches had fled, the old kings killing the magical for sport whenever the opportunity arose. It was one of the many things Fyia would change …

Fyia stepped down from the carriage, and a deep rumbling ground through the air. She looked up to see a metal ball drop out of the clock. The sound of metal on metal reverberated across the open piazza as the ball rolled down the copper runners. Fyia watched as it travelled down the left side of the building, then dipped into the water with barely a splash.

'Auspicious,' said a tall old woman, who was walking—spine ramrod straight—down the steps towards them.

'Stop,' said Fyia, starting up the stairs. 'We'll come to you.'

'I'm as fit as a fiddle, Your Majesty.'

'Even so …' Fyia climbed the endless stairs Sensis had lined with guards. The old woman sank into a deep bow when Fyia reached her.

'Spider,' said Fyia, 'it is good to see you.'

'And you, Your Majesty. If you'll come this way, the Extended Council has assembled.'

'The Viper's Nest,' said Sensis.

'That name is typically reserved for the Small Council,' said the Spider, with a stern look.

'Can't imagine it's much different,' said Sensis.

The building was ornately decorated, with mosaiced floors, patterned ceilings, and glassless windows. The city had been built long ago, when the lands had been warmer, when a frost this far south was virtually unheard of. Now, although not yet cold, the leaves only just beginning to turn, they still had need of their cloaks. Come the winter, the place would feel no warmth for three long cycles of the moon.

The Spider led them up a set of stairs, then along a wide corridor, where mechanical artwork lined the walls, making whirling, clicking noises as it moved. Fyia couldn't say she was a fan, not when she compared the artwork here to the wild paintings of her mountainous homeland.

'They're amazing, aren't they?' said Adigos, admiring a piece that depicted the movements of the sun.

'Hmm,' said Fyia, throwing him a questioning look. 'Not exactly what I was thinking …'

'Brace yourselves,' said the Spider. She paused before a set of huge metal doors covered with cogs of various sizes.

Fyia nodded, a seriousness descending over the group as they positioned themselves. The Spider pressed a hidden button, and a loud clanking filled the air, the cogs spinning as they swung inwards, revealing the council chamber beyond.

The chamber was vast, stretching all the way up to the clock tower above, some of the clock's internal mechanism visible. Towering columns ran down either side, and rows of stained-glass windows admitted muted light. Under the columns, lesser diplomats and courtiers lined the walls, and at the far end stood a long table, packed with expectant faces all craning for a look at their Queen.

Fyia held her head high, looking every inch the conqueror as she entered the chamber. Music began, floating across the air from somewhere at the back, and Fyia had to suppress a laugh at the shocked faces all around; evidently Rouel had snuck in ahead of them.

Fyia's wolves led the way, prowling towards the table, with Sensis and Edu—large and formidable—flanking her. Fyia surveyed the faces as she walked purposefully to the elaborate chair at the head of the table. Sensis and the Spider took the chairs to either side of Fyia, Edu and Adigos standing guard behind, her wolves sitting at her feet.

Fyia nodded to the Spider, who said, 'Your Majesty, with your leave, I bring this meeting to order. The members of your council would swear fealty.'

Fyia nodded. Her wardens—one for each of the five kingdoms—stood, bowed, and declared their loyalty, and then the rest of Fyia's Extended Council followed suit. Nobody missed the mocking edge from Lord Eratus Venir, the newly appointed warden of her most recently conquered kingdom. That he'd made it to her new capital before Fyia was impressive; he must have ridden hard from the Sky Kingdom.

'The next order of business,' said the Spider, 'is from Lady Lyr Patrice, the Warden of your homeland, the Starlight Kingdom.'

Lady Lyr stood, inclined her head to Fyia, then addressed the table. 'My lords and ladies, I petition the council for an increase in soldiers at the border between the Starlight Kingdom and the dark lands beyond.'

Fyia bristled. 'Those lands have names. The Land of the Fae'ch, and the Kingdom of the Black Hoods,' she said, looking Lady Lyr directly in the eye.

'Of course, Your Majesty,' said Lyr, clenching her teeth.

'What purpose would troops serve?' asked Sensis. As High Commander of Fyia's armies, her troops would be the ones to answer any such call.

'To protect against raiders,' said Lyr, 'and as a show of strength ... so they don't get any ideas.'

'So *who* doesn't get any ideas?' said Sensis, not bothering to hide her frustration.

'The Fae'ch, and the Black Hoods.'

'What ideas might they get?' asked Sensis.

'Ones about invading our lands ...'

'Has either given any indication they are considering an invasion? Have there been raids?' said Sensis.

'There have been rumors. We must be proactive ... not give them an opening.'

'Why would they want an opening?' said Sensis.

'I don't presume to understand the motivations of those ... people.'

Fyia clenched her fists under the table, reminding herself to be civil. The people of her homeland split into two broad camps: bigots and scaremongers who had an over-inflated sense of their own self-worth ... people like Lady Lyr, or Fyia's parents, and the progressives, like Fyia. Much as Fyia hated Lady Lyr and everything she stood for, the other bigots confided in her, so she had a use.

'Your request is denied,' said Fyia. 'You have no evidence of hostility, and no good will come from provoking our neighbors.'

'But ... Your Majesty ... the people of the Starlight Kingdom will not be pleased.'

'Do you mean to say ensuring harmony in the kingdom of my birth is outside your capabilities?' said Fyia.

Lady Lyr seethed, unable—or maybe unwilling—to hide her anger. 'I will, of course, do what I can …'

Fyia looked back to the Spider, ending Lyr's time. 'Lady Nara Orchus, of the Kingdom of Sea Serpents, and Lord Fredrik Feake, of the Kingdom of Plenty, would like to make a joint petition,' said the Spider.

Fyia turned her attention to the two figures rising from their seats.

'Your Majesty,' said Lady Nara, whom Fyia had always liked, 'Lord Fredrik and I are concerned about our trade prospects with the lands across the Kraken Sea.'

Fyia's kingdoms exported much to those lands, and the Kingdom of Sea Serpents shipped the goods to all the far-flung regions of the known world. Fyia inclined her head.

'We are concerned with the … ah … tense relations between Your Majesty and the Emperor across the sea,' said Fredrik. 'We fear trade will be adversely affected.'

He looked expectantly at Fyia, who said nothing. Instead, she held Fredrik's gaze until he continued. 'We would respectfully suggest Your Majesty explores a … uh … marriage contract with the Emperor, to secure peace and favorable trade agreements for the good of all five kingdoms.'

Fyia's gaze flicked between Nara and Fredrik. Maybe she wasn't as fond of Lady Nara as she'd originally thought …

'I will say this once, and once only,' said Fyia. Her tone caused the room to go still, and nervous tension permeated the air. 'I will never marry the Emperor, or anyone like him. I have not toiled for so long, risked so much, lost so many, only to give my kingdoms to a greedy, self-serving man. Especially a man with a reputation for brutality, who is harboring both my treasonous parents and many of the pitiful royals who fled my kingdoms at the first sign of their defeat.

'Trade is important—crucial—and will continue as it always has, whether or not I marry a foreign leader. They need our goods as much as we need theirs.'

'But, Your Majesty ...' said Fredrik.

Fyia waved her hand, halting his words. 'Fear not, Lord Fredrik, for I have work for you. I plan to make Selise the heart of my combined kingdoms. I intend to build a palace, which will act not only as my home, but more importantly, will become a center of trade for the world.

'We shall invite merchants to our lands. We will wow them with the treatment usually reserved for dignitaries, and then we shall make deals to secure good relations for generations to come.'

'I can only applaud such a vision,' said Fredrik.

'But to achieve our full potential, we must change the way things work,' said Fyia. The air went still once more, and Fredrik's face drained of all color. 'We will make the markets fair and accessible to all.'

Fredrik's mouth pinched. He and his peers had long run the markets like their personal playgrounds, demanding exorbitant taxes and giving prime spots to their friends.

'And all workers will be paid fairly across the Five Kingdoms.'

'Well ... I ... I'm not sure what you mean?' said Fredrik.

'Which part is unclear?'

'Workers are already paid.'

'You do not think everyone deserves *fair* payment for their work?'

'We should consult with the merchants, Your Majesty. These things are delicate ... should not be rushed ... especially if such action could hamper commerce.' Fredrik looked delighted with his argument, obviously thinking he'd found an excellent button to push.

'It is very simple,' said Fyia, her tone brooking no argument. 'As of the first day of the next cycle of the moon, any person wishing to operate in any market in any of my five kingdoms must pay all workers fairly—men and women. If they do not, they will be fined, and shall not be allowed to trade. I trust the two of you,' she indicated to Lord Fredrik and Lady Nara, 'can work out the finer details and enforce the new rules.'

Fyia nodded to the Spider, who moved onto the next item on her list, even though Fredrik and Nara still stood. 'Lord Sollow Antice, of the Kingdom of the Moon,' said the Spider. Fredrik and Nara finally returned to their seats.

'Your Majesty,' said Lord Antice, standing and bowing deeply.

Fyia gripped the arms of her chair. Gods give her strength ...

'We request you visit the Moon Kingdom,' said Antice. 'We should like to bestow on you an honorary degree from the university, and build a statue in your likeness to be placed proudly in the main atrium. It will replace the statue of the former King of Moon that stands today.'

Lord Sollow Antice had previously been Prince Sollow Antice, firstborn son of that very king. There was no love lost between the father and son, but that didn't explain his current motivation. He was too sweet by half ...

'Thank you, my lord.'

'There is but one other thing,' said Antice. Fyia nodded, unsurprised. 'I presume you need the services of the Guild of Architects to design your new palace? I would be delighted to summon our most accomplished members ...'

Fyia sat back in her chair. 'Remind me, Lord Antice, how many women are in that guild?'

Antice faltered, and Fyia didn't miss the flash of irritation in his eyes; not so sweet after all.

'The Guild of Architects does not admit women, Your Majesty.'

'How about your esteemed military academy? Or the healers' college?'

'As Your Majesty is aware, those institutions are only for men.'

Fyia gave him a long, hard look. 'Not any longer.'

Antice paled. 'You can't mean ...'

'I assure you, I can. Sensis will deal with the military academy. The Spider will compile a list of leaders for the healers' college and guilds. And my dear friend Essa Thebe—our most brilliant inventor— whom I have already asked to architect my new palace, will make a short list of candidates for Chancellor of the University.'

'Your Majesty!' said Antice, his fists balled at his sides. 'I must strongly advise against this. The people of Moon will consider it an attack on their way of life. It would not be an exaggeration to say we will see blood in the streets ...'

'You mean from the stampede of women rushing to register for an education that should have been available to them since birth?'

'No, Your Majesty, from the people who will lose their livelihoods. We will simply have too many workers ... it will throw off the balance.'

'Then admit fewer men,' said Fyia, 'although I very much doubt your words are true. Are we done?' Fyia looked at the Spider.

'One more petition, from Lord Eratus Venir, of the Sky Kingdom,' said the Spider.

Fyia's stomach dropped. *Wonderful.* She turned her eyes to the gnarled old man making a show of struggling to his feet. It was a façade; if he were truly so fragile, he'd never have made it here before her.

Lord Venir said nothing for a few moments, letting a vicious silence rip across the room that sank its claws into everyone present. As a representative of the most recently vanquished kingdom, he was somewhat of an unknown entity, and that made people nervous.

'Your Majesty,' he said eventually, with a deep bow, 'I have but one question.' He paused a beat, trying to intimidate her, but Fyia refused to be bullied. She looked at him with boredom in her eyes. 'Where are the dragons?'

A collective gasp went through the room. They'd all been thinking it, but apparently only Venir had the balls to ask out loud. Fyia respected him for that.

'They have not yet returned,' said Fyia, 'unless anyone present is harboring a dragon?'

Silence.

'Do you believe, Your Majesty,' Venir continued, 'the legend is false? That uniting the Five Kingdoms will not, in fact, bring back those beasts? Or maybe—and I say this with the greatest of respect—you are not the one destined for that path?'

Fyia's wolves snarled, and she felt Adigos and Edu tense behind her.

'Did you expect them to puff into being overnight?' asked Fyia, her tone mocking. 'Five eggs are all we have left, and the *Kings* outlawed magic.'

'They did no such thing,' said Venir.

'Yes, they did,' said Fyia, 'for everyone but a handful of men behind the walls of a secret guild. They chased away the Fae'ch—the custodians of magic, and Cruaxee, and fire-touch—even the priestesses of the Sea Serpent are forbidden to practice. As of this moment, I decree that magic is legal, and may be practiced by anyone who wishes. The knowledge held in the guilds and university will be freely shared.'

Antice and Venir spluttered unintelligible exclamations, but fell silent when Fyia turned fierce eyes upon them.

'The priestesses of the Sea Serpent will be delighted,' said Lady Nara. 'I shall send word to them immediately.' Fyia nodded in acknowledgement.

'It will be good for trade,' said Lord Fredrik, 'but will wipe out the existing black market. We'll have to watch for unrest on that front.'

'The Spider will see to that,' said Fyia.

Lady Lyr had gone pale. 'You're going to encourage those ... *people* to come back into our lands? This is the opposite of my request. The Starlight Kingdom will not stand for it.'

'You forget yourself, Lady Lyr. The Starlight Kingdom is *my* homeland. My people will welcome this news.'

'What of the dragons?' Venir asked again. 'What if they do not return?' Antice nodded in agreement, and he and Venir shared a meaningful look.

'They will,' said Fyia, her voice unwavering. *They had to.*

Chapter Three

THE SPIDER SHOWED FYIA and her entourage to an enormous townhouse after the meeting—Fyia's official residence in Selise until her new palace was ready. It had rooms enough to accommodate them all, as well as space for banquets and balls, and a garden that butted up against the river Sage, half a league before it merged with the river Empirisis. Empirisis flowed all the way from the Blue Mountains in the east, where it formed the border between Moon and Plenty, across Plenty's vast countryside, then through the Kingdom of Sea Serpents to the sea.

Fyia paced back and forth in front of the hearth in the large sitting room. The Spider sat on an uncomfortable-looking sofa, Adigos leaned against the frame of a floor-to-ceiling window, and Sensis lounged on a chaise longue, eating chocolate-coated strawberries.

'Gods, I'd forgotten how good these things are,' said Sensis, popping a strawberry into her mouth.

Fyia rolled her eyes, and the Spider tutted at the decadent display. Chocolate had become scarce since their lands had cooled, and eye-wateringly expensive.

'What will you do?' asked Sensis.

'The only thing I can do,' said Fyia. 'I know the location of only two eggs.'

'Fae'ch and Black Hoods?' said Sensis.

Fyia nodded. 'So off to the Fae'ch mountains I shall go.'

It wasn't an idea she relished, but she had no choice, and she longed to see her brother—an added bonus. Certainly the Fae'ch were the better of the two options, because with the Black Hoods, no one knew what was legend and what was true.

'You're running away?' said the Spider, with a cruel smile.

'I know that's how some will see it, but … convince them otherwise,' said Fyia.

'That's not my job,' said the Spider, 'and leading your council as your stand-in does not play to my skills.'

'Then who?' said Adigos. 'Sensis?'

Sensis laughed. 'The Queen's sending me to Moon to deal with the military academy, remember? And it's not a job for me either; military command and political councils are different beasts to tame.'

'I have to find the dragon eggs,' said Fyia. 'If I can't do that, it's only a matter of time before we have another war on our hands.'

'You're the legitimate ruler of the Five Kingdoms, even without dragons,' said Adigos.

'I know,' said Fyia, hotly, 'but not everyone sees it that way, especially given *your* actions during the war.'

'You know I'm sorry,' he said, his features betraying his guilt.

'You riled a few people up at the council meeting earlier, too,' Sensis said to Fyia.

'Rightly so,' said Adigos.

'It was stupid,' said the Spider, placing her hands calmly in her lap. 'You should have got them on side, and said you would consider marriage options. Only when they owed you something should you have introduced your ideas for the markets and guilds … slowly … step by step.'

'I will neither pander nor play politics,' said Fyia. 'If I start that way, I set the tone for my entire reign. But you're right, I need someone to keep them in line while I'm away.'

'There is only one person,' said Sensis, with a chuckle.

'You can't be serious …' said the Spider.

'She's right,' said Fyia. 'No one else is both capable and trustworthy.'

'She's a hedonist,' scoffed the Spider.

'Who?' said Adigos.

Fyia inhaled deeply, then held her breath. 'My aunt.' And convincing her would be a challenge.

It took a day's hard riding to reach the Temple of the Goddess. They tracked the river Sage and its adjacent canal upstream into the heart of the Kingdom of Plenty, but it was a beautiful autumnal day. Fyia smiled as she watched farmers working in the fields of the lowlands, tending to sheep and cows, or cutting late hay.

The Kingdom of Plenty provided much of the meat consumed within the Five Kingdoms, and it was good to see life continuing as normal, despite the war she'd brought to their doorstep. Plenty was the second kingdom she'd conquered, so they'd had time to adjust, and they were generally a good-natured, easy-going people. Unless she messed with the bloodlines of a prized variety of sheep, there wasn't much that would truly upset them.

The Temple of the Goddess was an imposing marble building that sat atop a square pyramid, with steps on all four sides. At the top, a terrace wrapped around, where the devouts of the temple regularly laid booby traps to prevent unwelcome visitors from making it inside.

Fyia paused at the bottom and looked up the steep stairs. A man wearing nothing but a loin cloth watched them, leaning against a pillar.

'I'll wait for you here,' said Edu, looking nervous. It was the first time Fyia had seen any hint of fear in his eyes.

She smiled, but didn't openly mock him in front of the guards. 'Everyone will stay here aside from me.'

'You're not going in there alone,' said Adigos. He flicked his pale blue eyes past Fyia to the devout at the top of the steps.

'You *want* to go inside?' said Fyia.

'It's too dangerous for you to go alone. What if someone attacks you?'

'The risk is minimal,' said Edu, 'but Adigos is right; we can't be too careful.'

Fyia chuckled, turning to walk up the steps, Adigos hot on her heels. 'Don't speak unless they ask you a direct question,' she said. 'Don't stare, keep track of your possessions at all times, and for Gods' sake, don't let them corner you.'

'You make it sound as though we're going into hostile territory. How bad can a bunch of old women be?'

'Oh, you sweet summer child.'

The man at the top bowed to Fyia and ignored Adigos—the shrine's devouts did not take kindly to other men.

Fyia stifled a laugh at Adigos' frown. *Just you wait* …

The devout led them through an atrium filled with light, channels of steaming water crisscrossing the floor. The temple sat atop a hot spring, hot water piped through every inch, so it was always at a temperature that allowed for barely any clothes.

They passed several naked devouts as they walked, Adigos stepping up beside Fyia, glaring at them all. Moans and gasps drifted out from the many alcoves, and Adigos' head whipped around, sending Fyia a look of disbelief. 'Don't they have rooms?'

'It's not a brothel,' said Fyia. 'You can wait outside if it's too much for your sensibilities. Really, you act as though you were born in Moon …'

'You know very well *this* is my homeland,' said Adigos, 'but not everyone in Plenty is quite so … liberal.'

'Maybe they should be.'

He looked aghast. 'They're not like this in your home kingdom …'

'Some of them are,' she said with a wink.

Adigos stuttered, searching for a response, but they reached a wooden section of wall, and the devout pulled a lever.

'Brace yourself,' Fyia whispered.

The wall tipped forwards, supported on either side by chains. It fell to the floor, where it formed a bridge across a particularly wide channel of water, and on the other side …

'*Sacred Warrior*,' muttered Adigos. He pulled Fyia back as she made to step onto the bridge. 'You cannot

214

be serious.' His face was inches from hers, his features almost pleading.

'Don't show weakness,' said Fyia, 'or you're done for.' She pulled out of his grasp and headed into the melee, the only word she could think to describe the debauched scene.

In the center of the space, three middle-aged women lounged on low couches, entirely naked. Each woman had three or four male attendants—all naked too—and were engaged in all manner of activities. One had a devout feeding her peeled grapes while her finger and toenails were painted, another received a massage, a man on each limb, and the third—her aunt—had one man's head between her breasts, and another kissing his way up her thigh.

'Starfall!' said Fyia, her voice an excited greeting.

Her aunt looked around, her features lighting up when she saw her niece. 'Fyia, darling, what a lovely surprise! Join in, by all means. And who is this delicious piece of man flesh?' she asked, eyeing Adigos. 'You should rid him of his clothes ... awfully hot in here.'

Adigos flinched.

'Oh ... you didn't bring a prude?'

'Leave if you're uncomfortable, Adigos,' said Fyia softly, sinking onto the couch next to her aunt. She beckoned one of the men to her side. Adigos went rigid as Fyia instructed the man to kiss her neck, then tipped her head back and let out a sigh. She hummed in appreciation as another gave her a foot rub.

Fyia watched Adigos as he watched her. She didn't miss the flaming fire of desire in his eyes. He'd always wanted her, since they'd first met, when she'd been sixteen and him twenty, her brother's best friend. She'd almost given in, just once, before he'd betrayed her for the first time. In another life, they would have been married … a life where her brother hadn't become Fae'ch …

Starfall clapped her hands, and the devouts got to their feet, then left the room. 'For Gods' sake, sit, Adigos. Don't think I don't remember you from your youth. You can't be shocked … not really … given what I recall of your exploits.'

'I'm not shocked,' he said. He sat next to the woman with drying nails. She leaned towards him, and he backed away, trying and failing to put distance between them.

'He smells nice,' she said.

Fyia stifled a smile. It was true; he did.

'So, Niece, what is it you want from me this time? I helped rid you of your parents, and I have my just reward,' she said, motioning around her, 'yet here you are again.'

'I have five kingdoms,' said Fyia.

'But no dragons,' said the woman who'd been having a massage, a glint in her eye.

'Or eggs?' said Starfall.

'You should find those,' said the woman next to Adigos. 'Not something to leave up to chance. May I …?' she said to Adigos, hovering a hand over his upper thigh.

'No,' said Adigos.

'Oh, good. I like them feisty.'

Adigos pursed his lips, small lines appearing on his brow. She wouldn't touch him without consent, but that wouldn't stop her from teasing him.

'But you can't leave your kingdoms shepherd-less,' said the first woman.

'You'll need someone you can trust …' said the second, mischievously.

'A safe and proven pair of hands,' agreed the first.

Starfall looked keenly at Fyia. 'So? How are you going to convince me when I have everything I need right here?'

'You expect me to believe that?' said Fyia. 'Look at the three of you, baiting me; you haven't had this much fun in years. I can practically see the cogs in your formidable minds spinning and whirling, calculating what you should demand of me.'

'We're *all* in on this?' said the first, as though the suggestion were ridiculous, but her keen eyes betrayed her interest. 'You only need one of us to lead in your absence … and you have the Spider. What purpose would we serve?'

'New positions are becoming available,' said Fyia.

'New positions?' said the second woman, leaning forward. 'Where?'

'Moon,' said Fyia.

'Moon,' repeated the woman, obviously weighing up the pros and cons.

'It's a shame we have such a wonderful life here,' said Starfall, with a shrug.

'You're a terrible liar,' said Fyia. 'Name your price.'

So they did. It was eye-watering: riches and accolades and property rights. They would most likely use none of it, the pleasure of the negotiation their true reward. It mattered not, for they were worth every copper, so after putting up a half-hearted fight, Fyia gave them all they asked.

'They stole my favorite dagger,' said Adigos. He complained to the Spider as they sat in the sitting room of Fyia's temporary residence.

'I told you to keep track of your possessions,' said Fyia, with a smirk.

'When will they arrive?' asked the Spider.

'Tomorrow. They're having a farewell party tonight.'

'I dread to think what that entails,' said Adigos.

'I bet they loved him,' said the Spider, sending Fyia a wide-eyed look.

'Like a cat loves a mouse,' said Fyia.

The Spider chuckled. 'I'll make preparations. Good night.'

The door clicked shut, and silence settled over the room. 'What did Starfall mean, about helping to get rid of your parents?' asked Adigos.

He moved to sit next to Fyia on a formal sofa, his bulk taking up most of the space. Warmth radiated off him, and she resisted the urge to reach up and play with his wavy blond hair. She craved the simple intimacy with a force that surprised her.

Fyia gave him a searching look. 'You know what happened.'

'I know you staged a coup, and had your parents bundled off across the Kraken Sea, but I didn't know Starfall helped.'

'You were with my brother, so I guess that makes sense, and few know what really happened.' Fyia could trust almost no one—she'd learned that the hard way—but there was no harm in telling Adigos now. 'After I refused my parents' edict to marry the Emperor across the Kraken Sea, I ran away. That meant, when I decided to overthrow them, I needed help from inside the castle.

'Starfall lived there, and invited my parents to her rooms one night for dinner. Her personal guards bound and gagged them, then carried them out through the secret passages. I went in the same way with my force, and took the castle without spilling a single drop of blood.'

'Why did she help you?'

'There was no love lost between her and my parents. My father was her younger brother, and Starfall was supposed to rule. My father pretended he had no interest in the throne, then organized a coup of his own, forcing a vote of no confidence in Starfall before she ever ascended the throne. She never saw it coming … that's what eats her up the most.'

'Didn't she want to rule herself once your parents were out of the way?'

'No. She'd never wanted it all that much anyway. She wanted freedom more … and revenge.'

'And hedonism,' said Adigos, raising an eyebrow.

'Nothing wrong with that,' said Fyia, a challenge in her eyes.

Adigos held her gaze, and the air went taut. A smile played across Fyia's lips; it had been a while since she'd enjoyed herself with a man, and Adigos had a lot to offer. She let her eyes roam across his broad chest, down his torso, across the bare, muscular forearm that rested across his thigh. She flicked her gaze back to his face: angular jaw, high cheekbones, light blue eyes, and her lips parted involuntarily.

He leaned in, invading her space, his eyes searching hers. His lips were achingly close, but he was hesitant. After everything that had happened, it wasn't surprising, but she didn't want him to hesitate. She wanted him to kiss her, take her, to have one place and time where her power and position didn't matter … to have an equal.

She lifted her fingers to his face, eyes on his lips, so close she could smell the whiskey on his breath. She shouldn't do it, not with him, not after everything, but she so wanted to … needed to. She skimmed her fingers over the prickle of his stubble, then ran her thumb across his lips. He parted them, gently biting the pad of her thumb before licking the skin with the tip of his tongue.

She closed her eyes against the sensation, desire pooling everywhere. She scraped her nails through his hair, and he sighed, leaning in so their cheeks touched. She rested against him, then exhaled sharply as he tugged her earlobe with his teeth. He lifted his fingers to her neck, caressing her with featherlight touches, then moved his lips, brushing them across the sensitive skin behind her ear. She tipped her head back, giving him all the access he wanted, her hand fisted in his hair.

The door clunked open just as Adigos finally got around to kissing her properly, sucking at her neck. He froze, and she let out a hiss of disappointment, her wolves growling as they approached.

'Your wolves were trying to get in,' said a light, female voice, '… oh, sorry, I can come back … wait, is that … Adigos? Okay, no, I'm staying.'

Adigos kissed Fyia's cheek, then pulled away, standing. 'Impeccable timing as always, Essa,' he said.

'It's so nice to see you too,' said Essa, cocking an eyebrow.

'I would hug you, but …'

'… Gods no,' said Essa, shuddering and circling a hand in the general direction of his nether regions.

'See you tomorrow,' said Adigos, sending Fyia a smoldering look.

Fyia lifted her head in acknowledgement.

'Your Majesty,' said Essa, bowing low. She was short, with dirty blond hair and a round, full face to match her curvy figure. Her grey eyes were sharp as knives, the juxtaposition striking. 'I would say I'm sorry, but I think I just saved you from yourself.'

'It's been a long time,' said Fyia, disappointment coursing through her.

'Since you saw me? Or since you indulged in carnal delights?'

'Both, but longer for the delights.'

'You can't be short on suitors?'

'I've had proposals, if they count, but no-one so bold as to propose anything less permanent, and I've been with the army; Sensis would string me up by my hair if I fooled around with her soldiers.'

'The trials and tribulations of being Queen.'

'Indeed,' said Fyia. She patted the space next to her on the sofa, and Essa sat. 'What about you?'

'Suitors?' said Essa.

'Or carnal delights?' said Fyia, with a grin.

'No,' said Essa. She shook her head, turning introspective.

'I'm sorry,' said Fyia. She put her hand on Essa's arm. 'It will ease in time.'

Essa gave a tight smile.

'My brother has a lot to answer for,' said Fyia. She leaned back against the sofa, raising her eyes to the intricate pattern winding its way across the ceiling.

'If he'd taken up his rightful position, you wouldn't be Queen,' said Essa.

'No, you would.'

'Of only a single kingdom, and I would've made a terrible queen ... I'm happy in my workshop.'

'Are you?'

'You know I am. Inventing is my only true love.' A shadow passed behind Essa's eyes; her only true love, aside from Fyia's brother ... 'I hear I'm to appoint a new Chancellor of the University?' she said, visibly forcing herself out of her reverie.

Fyia nodded. 'Apparently, I'm better at making enemies than enticing lovers to my bed.'

'The men of Moon may hate you for a while, but just think of all the women who can finally get an education ... and you can't make a clock without breaking an egg.'

'Do you really think they made the clocks with dragon eggs?'

Essa shrugged. 'That's how the saying goes.'

Fyia entered Essa's hastily assembled workshop at the top of the tallest tower in Selise. The sun was peaking over the horizon, rays of golden light punctuating the space. Four assistants bustled about, one measuring out brightly colored liquids, one hovering next to a bubbling pot, one taking a reading from a large solar simulation that hung from the ceiling, and one looking at the sky through a telescope. Essa was at a workbench, her face shielded with metal as she worked with a flame.

Essa didn't look up, so Fyia leaned against a bench and watched the activity. She could see the dragon clock through the window, a metal ball appearing at the top just as a ray of light illuminated the dragon's head. Such a mystery, how they worked, what they did ... She'd often wondered why the old Kings hadn't torn them down, against magic as they were.

Essa pulled off her shield and placed it on the bench. 'The Emperor across the Kraken Sea has created flying machines,' she said, leaving whatever she'd been working on to cool.

'What? How?'

'I don't know the details, or if it's really true, but we should send spies to gather intelligence.'

'Done,' said Fyia, 'but how do you know?'

'A trader,' said Essa. 'He supplies several inventors in the Kraken Empire. I've packed a few things for your trip.' Essa picked up a bag and handed it over. 'It's all the usual stuff; water purification, medicines, navigation devices, and a dagger that will stay sharp ... I found a new way to edge the metal, and added a special coating ...'

'Thank you.'

'And please will you deliver this to your brother?' She held out a small, perfectly round, perfectly smooth metal ball. It was almost gold, but with hints of other colors—pinks and blues and greens—just below the surface, catching the light.

'Essa ...'

'Don't judge me. Just take it, please.' Essa didn't meet her eyes.

'Okay,' said Fyia. The ball was small enough to fit in her palm, yet surprisingly weighty. 'Should I tell him anything when I give it to him?'

'No, thank you.'

Fyia didn't pry. They'd been friends for a long time, but Essa was a private person, and Fyia respected her privacy.

'Starfall will work with you on the stuff in Moon,' said Fyia, 'and Sensis will be there to ensure compliance.'

Essa nodded. 'We leave today. What about the plans for the palace? Who needs to see them?'

'Nobody. I trust your judgement, and you know what I want. The Spider or Starfall will help if you need anything.'

Essa nodded, then bowed. 'Safe travels, my Queen.'

Fyia pulled Essa into an embrace. 'You too.'

Fyia entered the council chamber, the members of her Small Council already waiting. Whereas the Extended Council included the wardens from each kingdom, as well as other key figures, the Small Council was less concerned with representation and more concerned with action. Every member of the Small Council played a crucial role, and Fyia expected them to be loyal to her first, and to their home kingdom or other interests second.

Along with Starfall, Sensis, and the Spider, who handled general leadership, the military, and intelligence respectively, she'd made two new appointments: Lady Nara Orchus of the Kingdom of Sea Serpents, to handle trade, and Lord Eratus Venir of the Kingdom of Sky, ostensibly to handle the kingdoms' finances, but also because Fyia wanted to keep an eye on him.

'You may by wondering why my aunt, Lady Starfall Orlightus, has joined us today,' said Fyia. The looks on Nara and Venir's faces said they knew exactly why Starfall was in attendance, but Fyia continued anyway. 'As you know, I am heading north, to the lands of the Fae'ch.'

'In search of dragons,' said Venir.

Fyia frowned, but he didn't even have the good grace to look abashed. 'While I am away,' she continued, 'Starfall will be my deputy. She has absolute authority in all things.'

'You're not worried she might betray you, as she did your parents?' asked Venir.

Fyia ignored him. 'While I am away, Sensis will travel to Moon, to reorganize the military academy. Nara will oversee the reformation of the markets, the Spider will appoint new academic and guild leaders, and Venir, you will ensure our coffers remain full upon my return.'

'Your Majesty,' they said together, accepting their tasks.

'Will you select a husband while you travel?' asked Lady Nara.

'You've given up on my marrying the Emperor so soon?' Fyia sniped.

Nara's cheeks colored. 'That was Fredrik's idea, not mine. I only wish you to marry *someone* ... there are no dragons, so ... and alliances would make us stronger ... enhance trade ...'

Venir interrupted Nara's stumbling words. 'Given the way King Milo was slain, not to mention the way you won your own home kingdom, you can't blame us for having questions.'

Adigos shifted almost imperceptibly behind Fyia. 'I can and will blame you for your questions,' said Fyia. 'I conquered all five kingdoms, and punished the men who snatched King Milo's kill from my hand.' Nara and Venir's eyes flicked to Adigos, Nara's eyebrows shooting up before she remembered to get them under control.

Fyia's wolves growled, and everyone at the table stiffened, even Starfall.

'Next time you question my right to rule, my Cruaxee will give you a permanent reminder of how badly you are mistaken.'

The air vacated the room, and a dark, foreboding silence settled. Nara and Venir averted their eyes.

'Venir, I am in need of a spy in the Kraken Empire. We've heard word they've invented flying machines.' A collective gasp filled the air. 'You will travel there, under the guise of a trade mission, and find out what you can.'

Venir flinched. 'But, Your Majesty, I have much to attend here ... my lands ...'

'Do not seek out my parents. If they try to contact you, ignore their request.'

Venir paled. 'But they're in the Emperor's palace … I may be unable to avoid them.'

'Then keep conversation to a minimum, or feed them lies … whichever you prefer. Act in accordance with the spirit of what I ask, and remember, the Spider's web is wide.'

Venir looked at her for a long moment, apparently speechless. 'Your Majesty,' he finally managed, bowing his head.

Fyia stood, and all at the table did so too. 'Starfall will take the meeting from here,' she said, nodding to her aunt. Starfall smiled, itching to get going.

'May the Gods protect you on your journey,' said Nara. 'I will pray to the Warrior to keep you safe from the Black Hoods.'

Fyia inwardly rolled her eyes; why was everyone so scared of the Black Hoods? 'I rather thought you might pray to the Whore, or I suppose the Goddess … anything to marry me off.'

'Your Majesty, I …'

'Hold your tongue, girl,' said Starfall. 'She's using you for sport.'

Fyia smirked as she left. 'May the Gods protect you all,' she called back over her shoulder. *For I fear you need it more than I.*

Kingdoms of Shadow and Ash is book one in the Shadow and Ash duology, and is available now through all major retailers.

ACKNOWLEDGEMENTS

A massive thank you to everyone involved in creating this (and all my books). To my awesome sister Alice, who reads early drafts, to my beta readers (especially Vela Roth for staging a rescue at the eleventh hour!), ARC and street team, BookTok and Bookstagram friends, Saint Jupiter for the beautiful covers, and of course, most importantly, to the wonderful readers who buy and recommend my books. Thank you!

And a huge thank you to the FaRoFeb Coven. For generally being awesome, openly sharing your secrets, and making our author community so delightfully fun.

CONNECT WITH HR MOORE

Check out HR Moore's website, where you can also sign up to her newsletter to read *The Water Rider and the High Born Fae* (a *Shadow and Ash* story) for free!
http://www.hrmoore.com/

Find HR Moore on Instagram, TikTok, and Twitter: @HR_Moore

Follow HR Moore on BookBub:
https://www.bookbub.com/authors/hr-moore

See what the world of *Shadow and Ash* looks like on Pinterest:
https://www.pinterest.com/authorhrmoore/kingdoms-of-shadow-and-ash/

Like the HR Moore page on Facebook:
https://www.facebook.com/authorhrmoore

Follow HR Moore on Goodreads:
https://www.goodreads.com/author/show/7228761.H_R_Moore

TITLES BY HR MOORE

The Relic Trilogy:
Queen of Empire
Temple of Sand
Court of Crystal

In the Gleaming Light

The Ancient Souls Series:
Nation of the Sun
Nation of Sword
Nation of the Stars

Shadow and Ash Duology:
Kingdoms of Shadow and Ash
Dragons of Asred (coming early 2023)

Shadow and Ash Stories:
The Water Rider and the High Born Fae
House of Storms and Secrets

http://www.hrmoore.com